THE COLOUR OF LOVE

SASKIA WOODHILL

Copyright © Saskia Woodhill

The author asserts her moral right to be identified as the author of this work.

PAPERBACK ISBN 978-1-73862-201-6

All rights reserved. No part of this book may be reproduced, stored in a retrieval system, or transmitted in any form or by any electronic or mechanical means including photocopying, recording, information or retrieval systems, or otherwise, without prior permission in writing from the publisher, with the exception of book reviewers, who may quote short excerpts in reviews.

A catalogue record of this book is available from the National Library of New Zealand

Lightpool Publishing

www.lightpoolpublishing.com

PROLOGUE

*L*ater Julia would look back on that turbulent time, those few autumn months when so much seemed to be crammed into a short period of time and her life changed dramatically. When a series of unconnected events combined to steer her in a different direction and utterly change her future.

She could never have imagined that a minor accident would set in train a sequence of events that would change everything in so many ways. Sometimes she mentally listed all the random things that had happened in barely three months: the accident itself and the new friends she had made because of it, the stalker in the red car and the pervert she had reported to the police, and how she had subsequently become stuck with him in a stalled, dark lift. And last but not least the sarcastic man to whom she felt pulled as if by

1

a gravitational force despite the disdain he felt for her.

But the most surprising thing of all was how love came out of left field, tackled her to the ground before she saw it coming and held her down until she admitted to herself that the person she had fallen in love with, suitable or unsuitable, was destined to be the love of her life, the person she wanted to wake up next to every morning until old age claimed them both.

On crisp and sunny autumn day with a faint hint of winter in the air, Julia arrived at work early hoping to sort out a problem with a vital box of VW parts that the couriers seemed to have misplaced somewhere along the line. She parked at the back of the big workshop and clicked the security system remote before she even got out of the car, the way she always did now. The horrific assault on her eardrums a year ago when she opened the door immediately after using the remote, was still vivid in her mind. The way the internal siren echoed through the huge space, bounced of concrete floors and walls, made her ears ache, and nearly gave her a heart attack was not an experience easy to forget.

Once inside the cold, high ceilinged space she looked around her domain, and checked that everything had been turned off and put away the night before when she had left ahead of the senior mechanic, who was staying late to do some repairs to his own car. But she should have known that Rob would never leave a mess to be tidied up the next day. They had worked together for years, three as employees in a big place on the other side of town, and then Rob had joined Julia when she set up her first two-bay workshop, initially with only herself as mechanic, office worker and cleaner.

She had only been in that situation for less than a year when Rob turned up one evening, just as she was ready to lock up very late after a long and exhausting day and asked if she needed someone to work alongside her.

'I want a change,' he had said and smiled that tight little smile of his. 'I want to work in a different environment and be left alone to do a good job and be trusted.' He ran his hand over his buzz cut grey hair as he always did when he felt embarrassed, a gesture she knew well. 'It doesn't feel right to me that I've been in that place for nine years now and they still sometimes ask me to double check some things I've just done, as if I was a newbie, not someone with twenty-five years' experience.'

Julia had accepted him with open arms. She had never worked out if her business had grown so fast and got so busy because she was the only woman mechanic in town, but it wasn't only women who brought their cars to her, so that probably wasn't the main reason. Maybe it was just that the city was growing, and things were getting busier generally, so there weren't enough workshops to cope with the work. But whatever the reason it was good for business and as her customer base continued to grow it enabled her to expand and add two more workshop bays and employ more mechanics. These days she very rarely helped in the workshop herself but spent most of her time dealing with customers, running the accounting and ordering systems and being the front person behind the reception desk.

Now, she went through to the office, turned on the lights and booted up the computer before she hung her jacket behind the door and checked her hair in the mirror. She looked critically at the canary yellow shirt she hadn't worn once since she bought it several weeks ago and decided it was a good colour after all. Her sister Barb always said that Julia could wear any colour at all with her colouring, but sometimes she wondered if wearing bright colours drew too much attention to her as a person. Maybe having masses of black, curly hair wasn't so eye-catching in itself, but combined with striking colours it made her stand out. Never mind, she told herself, just be yourself. Nobody expects a woman working in a garage to look like a business executive.

But she couldn't waste time thinking about her shirt today. Why the order from the big parts warehouse in Penrose hadn't arrived was a mystery. At their end they had the proof they had sent it, the courier company's tracking system confirmed it had been delivered, but it had never arrived and now it was urgent. A customer was waiting for a car they needed for a holiday trip, and she knew she'd lose them if the car wasn't ready on time. The cancellation late yesterday afternoon for an early morning booking today was a blessing because it would give her a chance to spend some time tracking down the parcel. If it had been delivered to another garage by mistake she would have time to pick it up, while one of the men manned the office. If she couldn't locate it she would try the other garages in town in case they had the spare part she needed in stock, in which case they might let her buy it.

An hour later she had located and picked up the missing parcel from a garage in a suburb, and the workshop was noisy with tools clattering on hard surfaces and the radio on. Julia was so engaged in what she was looking at on her computer screen that she didn't immediately realise a man had come in until she suddenly sensed someone standing by the counter and looked up. He wasn't an existing customer, and she immediately switched to what the mechanics called her customer face. If she was in the workshop when a customer drove into the forecourt one of the guys would say, 'Quick, Julia – get your customer face on!'

'Sorry! I was so busy trying to solve a problem, I didn't hear you come in. What can I do for you?'

'I'd like my brake light connection looked at,' he said with a slightly sarcastic look and Julia wondered if the expression was caused by her admission that she had a problem or if there was something about her he found ridiculous; maybe it was the yellow shirt.

'Of course,' she said cheerfully, because she was never one to show what she felt, and her customer face was the armour she carefully kept in place when dealing with difficult people. 'Would you like it done right now? We had a cancellation for a half hour slot this morning, so we could do it right away if you can wait.'

'Yes, please,' he said. 'Should I drive it in now? I noticed there was one space empty.'

'We prefer to have our staff drive vehicles into the workshop, so if you give me the keys I'll organise that. And what's the problem with the brake-lights?'

'Only one side works on a trailer when I connect it, the right side and the fault isn't in the trailer light.'

'OK, you're welcome to help yourself to a coffee in our customer lounge through that door over there while you wait. Biscuits in the glass jar, just help yourself. Can I have the key please?'

He handed her the key and again she noticed that fleeting look of sarcasm, then he turned and disappeared through the door to the customer lounge. Julia went out to drive his Ford Ranger utility truck, black as was the current trend, into the empty service bay, told Morgan what was wrong and returned to the office.

Twenty minutes later she was taking a phone call when Morgan poked his head around the door from the workshop, handed her a key fob and pointed to the front yard where the black truck was now parked. He made a thumbs-up signal and retreated.

Standing in the door to the customer lounge, Julia studied the sarcastic customer for a moment before she spoke. He was engrossed in reading something on his phone, an attractive man in his mid or late forties with thick dark hair, fit looking and slightly tanned.

'The brake light connection's fixed,' she said, and he looked up. 'Here's the key. Would you like to pay as a casual customer, or would you like to be entered into our database of regular customers?'

He hesitated for a moment, got up and followed her to the counter. 'Put me in the database, please. I've had a couple of issues at the place I normally go to, maybe it's time for a change. All my details are here.'

She took the card he handed her and glanced at the name, Milton Parker. 'And the registration number, please, so we can send a reminder about the warrant of fitness. I can't see the plate from here. The reminders usually go out a fortnight before the due date, but if you want longer advance notice we can set it up.'

What a pity he gets that sarcastic look on his face whenever he looks at me, thought Julia and processed the payment, thanked him and remained standing to watch him leave. A handsome beast, gorgeous actually, but that sarcastic look! He wasn't openly rude or condescending, and she was sure he had no idea that his hidden attitude showed on his face. He smiled and there it was, that little sarcastic tweak. And then she laughed and told herself she'd better get used to it if he was going to be a regular, though what it was about her that caused his reaction was a mystery and not something she was used to.

At half past five Julia parked at the supermarket on the southern side of the central business district, where the suburbs became rougher the further south you went then gradually morphed into the only area in the city that could be described as crime ridden. She walked three blocks to Ben's Bistro where she was meeting Helen, and as usual she found her parking decision had been right. There were no empty parking spaces anywhere near the bistro and she would rather walk along the well-lit thoroughfare from the supermarket than park in one of the dark side streets in this part of town. As an additional bonus the carpark at the supermarket was well lit, so she wouldn't get her lovely new car key-scratched, as had happened to Helen a couple of weeks ago.

But why did Helen always suggest they met here? OK, this had been a regular hang-out when they were young, but that was before the area started going downhill. There were far nicer places closer to the centre and safer places to park. But walking in the dark was a favourite thing of Julia's, so she didn't really mind. The evening was chilly with a light breeze from the mountain ranges to the west, a foretaste of winter, when the winds off the snow often kept the city hostage for days on end. But tonight, it was invigorating, and Julia buttoned her coat and turned up the collar. Maybe enjoying a brisk walk in the chilly near dark demonstrated that she was still a country girl at heart; most of her friends would avoid it if they possibly could. Her childhood had been spent in an isolated house half an hour outside the city, close to the braided river and surrounded by native forest.

The dusk had deepened to near dark since she left the garage, and she was the only pedestrian to be seen, but on this busy arterial route she felt safe even in this rundown part of town, at least at this time of the evening when people we're still heading home from work, and there was plenty of traffic in both directions. She knew that Helen would probably have parked her car on one of the side streets if she hadn't found a space right outside the bistro. She always seemed to arrive early and didn't seem to worry about the possibility of getting her car keyed again.

The bar was warm and inviting with strings of bud lights suspended along the walls and over the counter. Helen was at a table on the far side with two glasses of something pink in front of her and watched Julia approach with a wide smile on her round face.

'What have you got there?' Julia hung her coat of the back of a chair and sat down before she ran her fingers through her hair to untangle the windblown locks. 'Pink gin?'

'Very special gin, botanical gin.' Helen held her glass up and studied it affectionately. 'Flavoured with flower petals, maybe roses, so gorgeous. I haven't had a gin in years, not since we were in our twenties, I don't think, but I spotted this lovely bottle with pastel coloured flowers all over it and asked the barman what it was.'

'And ordered two before you'd even tasted it because it came in a pretty bottle?'

'Don't be silly! One for me and one for you. It's delicious - I asked for one part gin and three parts tonic the way we used to drink it way back then.'

'You're right, it's gorgeous,' said Julia when she had tasted her drink. 'You can really taste that light flower flavour. So, miss Bingley, what have you been up to apart from discovering new gin flavours? And probably flirting with the barman, knowing you.'

'Are you ever going to stop calling me miss Bingley? I mean, how long is it since we read Pride and Prejudice? Probably second to last year of high school and ever since my surname has been a joke amongst our friends.'

'Just a habit, Helen, sorry! It was your surname until you married, after all, no harm intended - I'll make an effort to stop doing it. Please note I never use your Girl Guide tribal name from when we did that tramp in the ranges. Why you picked Wolf I can't imagine. Anyone less like a wolf would be hard to find.'

'I have no idea. It's too long ago and whatever I thought at the time must have been slightly mad. Wolf is more a man's name, I think. Perhaps I was being sarcastic about my chubby self.'

Julia grinned. 'Talking about sarcastic - let me tell you about a guy who thinks he has stealth sarcasm honed to a fine art and absolutely *no* idea that it shows on his face. Today this sexy beast of a guy, about forty-five or so, came in. I'd never seen him before, so I apologised for not having noticed him for a moment - I was sorting out a minor stock problem at the time. And he gave me this little smile, meant to look semi-friendly, but I saw the little tweak of the eyebrow, so then I watched for it, and every time he spoke to me it was the same - *every* time.'

'You didn't have oil or grease on your face, did you, like you do sometimes? It's a bit disconcerting when you've got your smart office gear and make-up on, and a big black mark smeared down your cheek like you did last time I brought my car in.'

'No, I checked – no marks anywhere. And how *is* your car now we've fixed that complicated technical problem?'

'Ha! Sarcasm seems to be catching, but it's fine, thanks. Why I didn't think to put a new battery in the fob when it wouldn't lock or unlock, I can't imagine.'

Julia grinned. 'One reason is that you had turned off the function that warns you about things like that – or someone had, because it should have come up on your screen. And you probably don't have a screwdriver small enough to open the fob anyway. We don't' mind doing little helpful things, you know that. And the new boy thought you were luscious, did I tell you? I heard him talk to the others after you'd gone – he was quite expressive, probably because he didn't know I was listening.'

'God, not that skinny little chap who looks like he's sixteen or seventeen? How embarrassing – I could be his mother.'

'Embarrassing? Are you mad? It's flattering that he even noticed a woman who's on the wrong side of forty - just. And talking about age, did I tell you Diane is expecting twins after all these years of saying she's not interested in having children? I thought I'd never have any nieces or nephews from her, and now I'll have two at the same time. I'll have to make a trip to Hawke's Bay when they've arrived. But let's get some bar food, I'm starving. And why are you out having a drink in a bar on a weekday anyway? What are Dave and the boys doing?'

'They're at a rugby match, Craig's playing for the school for the first time and he's particularly excited about it because they're playing under lights – God knows why, but it seems to be something they all get excited about. We'll have a late dinner when they get home, it's all prepared. It just seemed like a perfect opportunity to see you now that my weekends are so loaded with sports. Isn't it weird? There's not a single person in our extended families who's a rugby fan, we're all into football, and now both boys have taken up rugby. Must be the school they're at.'

Julia smiled and decided to change the subject to avoid another half hour discussing whether Helen should have given in to her husband about sending the boys to an all-boys high school. They had talked about this several times and as far as Julia was concerned there was nothing further to be said.

'Let me tell you what I just read on the Guardian webpage this morning,' she said as a diversionary tactic. 'There's a book club in the US where they've read the same book for twenty-eight years, Finnigan's Wake. Remember our English teacher said he had started it three times and never got past the first few pages?'

When they parted outside an hour later, Helen turned just as she was about to walk away to her car, which was parked on a side street as usual. 'I do like the way you do your hair now, it's gorgeous. I was going to say it when you first came in, and then we got side-tracked talking about the gin. How do you get those big loose curls?'

'All thanks to Mr Dyson's clever device that curls and blows hot air through your hair at the same time, believe it or not. It turns my boring natural curls into something a bit trendier in no time at all. *And* it revolves so it winds up your hair on the cylinder thing while you just stand there and hold it. Not that I'd ever imagined I'd buy one of those things, but Barb put me on to it when I was having a moan about my hair.'

'For God's sake! You've got lovely hair anyway, you always did – but you've taken it to the next level now. Bye, got to run or I'll be late!'

Julia had only just closed her apartment door and taken her coat off when Gwyneth called and asked if she'd like a game or two of Scrabble, so she picked up a bottle of red wine, some cheese and a packet of crackers and went next door.

An hour and half later after losing two games, Julia was reaching across to fold the board and lift it to pour the letter tiles back in the cloth bag Gwyneth was holding up, when she nudged her wineglass and a splash of red wine spilt over the board.

'Shit!' Julia looked around for something to mop it up with before it ran over the edge of the table and onto the carpet.

'Don't panic!' Gwyneth pushed what remained of the cheeses off the napkin on the tray beside her and dabbed at the wine while Julia raced to the kitchen to grab paper towels.

'I think it's ruined,' she said a few minutes

later. 'I'm so sorry! Look, the paper surface is peeling off. I never noticed that your board had paper stuck on, I thought it was the same as mine with everything printed directly onto the board.'

Gwyneth pushed the edge of paper that was lifting, and a piece came off and stuck to her finger. 'This set's ancient, I got it when I was a teenager, so it's sixty years old. Time I got a new one anyway, I like your plastic tiles much better than these wooden ones. I'll get a new one next week when I go to the doctor for my checkup.'

'Oh no, you won't!' Julia started wiping everything down with the paper towels. I'll get you one – or maybe I'll get two, so I can take one to Barb's place and play Scrabble with her kids. They need dragging away from their huge collections of Lego now and then.'

An hour later Julia was curled up in her favourite armchair reading when she heard her phone ping with a text message and ignored it until she had finished the chapter before she picked her phone up to see who sent her a message at that time of night. She glanced at the screen and made a face when she saw the name of the sender. Stuart was her ex-partner, whom she had left a couple of years earlier when she could no longer put up with his controlling personality. The message said *Up for a drink sometime soon?* She didn't reply.

. . .

Her affair with Stuart had begun as a casual dating relationship. He was newly divorced and renting a flat while he looked around for something to buy. But his short term lease ran out before he had found anything he liked enough to buy, and he asked if he could move in with her. Call it temporary roommates, he had said initially, and she had taken him at his word and to start with it seemed to work. He slept in the spare bedroom, but after a while the dating relationship cum roommate arrangement turned into something different, something more serious and more permanent feeling, a real relationship.

It wasn't long before she started wondering if she had made a mistake. Stuart gradually displayed more possessive and controlling characteristics, something that hadn't been obvious when they started dating and lived separately. She never worked out if he had concealed his true character, careful to present a good image, or if she just hadn't picked up on it before they were living in the same apartment.

After nearly two years she broke it off, and she would never forget the period after the breakup. Constant calls and messages, taunts and recriminations and occasional outbursts of emotion when he turned up on her doorstep and promised to be different if they could only continue as a couple. She had no experience of men like him; there had been nobody like it within her own extended family, and she had never dated anyone of that kind, but she knew more about it now. Talking to others and reading about it had taught her that men who did this, who manipulated a woman to make her feel inadequate, caused hurt and then promised to reform, were not to be trusted. They would invariably do the same thing over and over and expect to be forgiven. They either thrived on the circular process of emotional upheaval or were incapable of changing their behaviour. She turned her phone off without responding.

Julia's two younger sisters, Diane and Barb were as different as chalk and cheese. Diane lived in Hawke's Bay and often seemed to disapprove of Julia in a subtle way that made having a close relationship with her slightly difficult. Barb, the youngest in the family, had always been close to Julia and often asked for her opinion even though they were utterly different. When Julia drove to Barb and Anthony's place for coffee that weekend she wondered if she would have a chance to ask her advice about something so personal that she hadn't been able to bring it up in a phone call. It had to be discussed face to face, but she would need to be alone with Barb to talk about it.

As she swung in and parked behind Anthony's car on the street outside their house she studied the uneven path to the front door with a frown.

Why on earth didn't they just fix it? she thought, as she reached into the back seat for the children's present and her bag. One day someone would break a leg and it was easy to fix. She opened the little gate and stood for a moment studying the path. 'I reckon Anthony and I could do it in a morning,' she said out loud to herself, 'it just needs some of those concrete pavers lifted and the ground under them evened out, maybe a couple of bags of sand.' She walked to the front door in a hop-and-step way to avoid tripping that she had got used to since they moved in.

'Not another present for the kids!' exclaimed her sister with mock horror when Julia handed the parcel with the Scrabble box to nine-year-old James. 'Honestly, Julia - you've got to stop spoiling them, it's getting embarrassing. You can't bring presents every time you come.'

'What do you think, James?' said Julia without responding to Barb. 'Do you think I'm spoiling you or do you think I just enjoy giving you things?'

'I think you enjoy making us happy,' said James without hesitating and Barb laughed. 'I give up – how could I possible enforce a no-present rule and make my kids unhappy?'

They spent an hour playing Scrabble with the children after an inspired rule change instigated by Barb, to avoid six-year-old Debbie being disadvantaged.

'Here's the rule for when you play with people still at primary school,' she said breezily as if this was a long-established thing. 'No words longer than five letters and we take out the letter Z and the letter Q.'

Halfway through the game Debbie looked at the board and said, 'You know what? We're making a crossword.' She giggled. 'If you take a photo of it when we're finished we could make up the clues and send it to the newspaper – they have one every day, I've seen it when I look at the comic strip. We do little crosswords at school – tiny compared to this.'

The sisters exchanged a glance of surprise, and Julia smiled at Debbie. 'Great idea - let's do that. Maybe we could print out the grid and make up the clues, and you could take it to school.'

One game was enough before the children drifted off outside and left Julia to broach the subject that had sat in the back of her mind all week. With a second cup of coffee in her hand, she turned sideways on the sofa and looked seriously at her sister.

'I want to talk to you about that young guy I told you about a couple of months ago, the welder - Ashton. I don't know if I should go out with him or not, but he keeps asking. It seems nearly indecent to date someone his age.'

'Really? Does anyone say that about a man who goes out with a younger woman?' Barb made a face. 'When a man dates a woman who's much younger, most people give him credit for being cool and having what it takes, so why doesn't the same thing apply to women? And how old is he anyway?'

'He's a lot younger than I am, nineteen years to be precise. The first time he asked, I said no thanks and told him I'm too old for him. It turned out he had my age wrong by about ten years, so he hadn't realised the age gap was as big as it is. But he's persisting, came in for a warrant of fitness for his truck the other day and asked me again, he says he doesn't give a shit that I'm so much older – his words, not mine.'

'Is he nice looking?'

'God, yes - hot as!' Julia laughed. 'Just gorgeous and sexy, and he has a marvellous smile. He could melt an iceberg in five seconds. Do you think I should have an affair with him until he gets tired of me? It's not as if it could ever be a lasting thing, but I don't want his mates to tease him, he's a nice, quiet guy. Remember how mum would say someone was either couth or uncouth. This guy's definitely couth, if there really is such a word.'

'Of course, you should go out with him!' Barb gave her a sly smile. 'I would if I were you. And who cares about the age thing – if you like him enough you can have a nice little fling and then he'll go off with someone younger and have a family and just be a friend and customer. Or maybe you'll last forever. I've heard of stranger things.'

And there the conversation about Ashton ended when Anthony walked in. 'Hi,' he said. 'I thought I'd be a couple of hours longer than this, but the problem wasn't as complex as they thought, very simple in fact. But who cares, they called me in and I'll get paid.'

'What was it?' Julia was always interested to hear about Anthony's various maintenance contracts and the issues he had to deal with, mainly specialised issues that were interesting. They were the only two people in the extended families on either side who were into mechanical and technical things, and Barb sometimes threatened to leave the table and eat in the kitchen if they didn't stop what she called mind-numbingly boring conversations over dinner.

Anthony paused on his way to the kitchen. 'Go to YouTube and check out that Machinery Magazine channel I told you about – they've got a new video up about the latest MillPro trimming line. They built a huge new building out at the mill to house the new line a few months ago, so I'm out there now and again making little adjustments – this time it was just a guiding bar that was getting stuck, so it was easily fixed. They thought it had something to do with the automation which their guys don't touch, but it was minor. They run it twenty-four hours a day, six days a week, so it had to be fixed even though it's Saturday. Sunday's the only day they close the mill.'

'I hope there's someone out there you can teach how to do these minor fixes,' said Barb. 'This is the second weekend in a row you've had to go out there.'

'That's just what I do each time, I make sure the shift foreman knows how to fix it, or their machinery maintenance guy, if he's there - unless it's something really complex, but I haven't struck anything major yet. It's a very well made machine, top quality. And those adjustments are mostly simple - you could do them if I showed you how.'

He directed a sly smile at Barb, who made a hideous face back. 'God, no! I keep well clear of machinery and technical things.'

Julia drove home deep in thought about the Ashton dilemma, debating with herself if she should take Barb's advice or not. On the one hand it was tempting; she hadn't had a regular date for a couple of years, not since she broke up with Stuart, and Ashton was a lovely young guy, but then? How would it end? And did she want to take the risk?

She thought back to the dramatic time of liberating herself from her relationship with Stuart and knew she had to be careful not to get into anything again that might end badly. The reverberations from the Stuart debacle had been exhausting and thinking about it still made her feel unsettled. But Ashton was kind and soft spoken, not to mention very sexy and he had a great body. She felt sure he couldn't possibly turn out to be the controlling, abusive kind.

3

ob was sitting at Julia's desk in the
office when she returned after
another urgent dash to pick up a courier parcel
of parts that had once again been delivered to the
garage on the far side of town,

'Great – I need that,' he said and came around
the counter to take the big box from her. 'And
what the hell is the problem with the courier
drivers, dropping our stuff off at the wrong
place? But listen, we've just had a real weirdo in -
very weird. He's just paid and left, or you could
have met him yourself.'

'Weird how?' asked Julia and hung her jacket
behind the door connecting the reception area to
the garage and checked her hair in the mirror, a
habit that had only developed since she started
seriously styling her hair.

Rob paused and rested the box on the corner

of the counter. 'He came in, wanted his brake lights checked and the passenger seat in his truck was full of tech gear – lots of it. Two open laptops propped up at an angle and all kind of other stuff I don't even know the name of on the floor and on the dashboard – never seen anything like it. Cables all over the place.'

'Probably someone who runs their business from their car. Like the guy in that Netflix series – The Lincoln Lawyer. Did you see it? Great show!'

'I don't think so,' said Rob. 'Not this guy - a big, rough guy, scruffy and dirty looking – and with a car full of expensive looking gear. And in use too, in the car – those laptops were on, the screens were lit up.'

He left with the box of parts and Julia resumed what she'd been doing before they discovered another delivery had gone missing and forgot the conversation about the weird guy.

Early that evening when she was just about to turn the computer off after checking that the weekly cloud backup was set up, Rob entered the office with the new mechanic in tow.

'What are you guys doing here?' said Julia, who hadn't realised someone else was still in the building. 'You should have gone home half an hour ago - is there some kind of problem?'

Rob looked troubled. 'Might be, but Shane had better tell you himself what he saw - I think you should know. We've been sitting in the lunchroom discussing it, but I think you should decide how we handle this.'

Alerted by the serious look on Rob's face Julia swung around on her chair. 'OK, let's hear it, Shane.'

It was obvious that Shane had trouble getting started. Looking down at the floor he hesitated for a few moments while Rob and Julia waited silently, then he looked up. 'Rob says he told you about the weirdo with the tech gear in his car. He didn't see what was on those screens, but I did. I was working on a car that was up on the hoist on the other side and ...' His expression was half-guilty. 'I wasn't trying to look or anything, I just turned and stood there for a moment wiping my hands on a rag, so I was right beside that guy's driver's door – I couldn't help seeing the screen facing me and I thought it was strange. The screen on my laptop shuts down if nothing happens for fifteen minutes or something.' He frowned. 'And why does someone drive around with two laptops turned on and working? It seemed really weird. So, I had a closer look and noticed all the other stuff in that car.'

'And? What did you see? Clearly something that makes you uncomfortable, Shane. Just tell us, so we can discuss what we should do about it.'

He stopped for a moment and looked as if he would rather not tell her. He feels guilty, thought Julia, as she watched his troubled face. He's young enough to mix up cause and effect, he needs some help.

'Well thank goodness you did notice,' she said, 'because whatever it was you saw must be important, and if you hadn't spotted it perhaps nobody would.'

'He's got live images of toilets - he's filming women in toilets.'

'Christ! Like live-streaming somehow to his car? Which means he's got cameras planted in the toilets. He must have left the laptops open by mistake.'

'I know, creepy as hell,' said Shane, feeling more confident now and looking more relaxed. 'You'd think he would have closed the laptops, wouldn't you, but he just jumped out and walked straight into the workshop and talked to Rob and he went out and dove the truck in right away– we had a space. The guy's a plumber, it says on the doors of the truck, so he'd have the opportunity to set things up, wouldn't he?'

'And what you saw was live?'

'The screen had several images, you know, like yours does when you look at security camera footage, and in one a woman was standing, pulling her pants up. I'm sure that one at least was live, but I didn't stay beside the truck very long. I moved away a bit, so he wouldn't catch me staring.'

'Where was he? In the customer lounge?'

'No, he'd left the truck and gone somewhere.' Shane looked at Rob. 'Didn't you say he'd gone down the road to the get something to eat?'

Rob nodded. 'He was in a hurry, but a cop had seen him at the petrol station and told him to get his brake lights fixed. He said he'd be back in half an hour - he was going to get a burger from MacDonalds. When Shane told me what he saw I thought we'd better tell you straight away.'

'So, he didn't see you looking? He came back and drove off?'

'Yeah, he just paid and left. And he'd want to get his lights fixed,' said Rob. 'A guy with that sort of stuff in his car wouldn't want to get pulled over by the cops, would he?'

Julia tried to imagine why Shane hadn't told anyone as soon as he noticed what was on those screens instead of waiting several hours, but he was very young, and maybe he wasn't comfortable being what he might term a snitch. She couldn't quite put herself in his place. Eighteen-year-old males were a mystery, she thought, but at least he'd told her now. She made up her mind to have a chat to him sometime about life in general and check how clued up he was.

Julia swung her chair to face the computer.

'Let's get the truck up on the security camera. I'd like to have a look at this guy. Has he been here before?'

'Never saw him in my life till today,' said Rob. 'He just paid as a casual and left, he'd just gone when you came back with that parcel. And I'd be just as happy if he didn't come back, I didn't like the way he talked to me. A bully, I'd say.'

'OK, let's have a look at that footage. So, he must have got here just after I left - let's start at quarter past twelve.'

With Rob and Shane crowded in behind her Julia pull up the footage from the security cameras.

'There he is!' Shane pointed at the top left corner of the screen where the camera which filmed the forecourt showed a white utility truck driving in. 'That's him – you can see the logo on the door, it's green and black in real life.'

Julia made a note of the registration plate, and they watched the driver get out of the cab and disappear into the open service bays, then walking away towards the street while Rob got into the truck and moved it.

'So, what now?' Rob took a step back. 'Do we call the cops?'

'Let's see what we can show them,' said Julia. 'Let's follow the camera that films inside the workshop.'

'Why?' asked Shane. 'Does it matter?'

'Perhaps not, but if we get a shot of you looking into the truck from the driver's side it kind of proves you did see something. And maybe it will show whose laptops on the seat. It would be great if we could prove they were there, wouldn't it?'

Images on the quadrant of the screen that showed the inside of the workshop came up and disappeared, dozens of short clips when the camera was activated by someone appearing from behind a vehicle or straightening up from bending over an engine.

Then the big guy appeared, talked to Rob and left with Rob following him outside. Next the white truck drove in and Rob got out. Julia stopped the video and zoomed in on the truck and they all leaned forward.

'Yep,' said Rob. 'See those lines forming a V-shape? That's the top of the screens sitting at an angle. Pity we can't see right down to the seat.'

Julia started the playback again and after a few moments Shane appeared from under the car on the hoist.

'There!' said Rob and Julia stopped the video then went forward slowly. 'There you are, Shane – and look at the way you kind of stop mid-step and lean forward. It's obvious you saw something that caught your attention.'

In the black and white clip, they watched Shane stand still for a moment wiping his hands, then lean closer to the driver's window of the truck. Suddenly he looked towards the forecourt and quickly moved away.

'That's when I suddenly thought of that big guy coming back and catching me looking,' said Shane. 'Shit - I hate to think what he'd do to me if he knew I'd seen those images. He looks mean. But why did he leave them open like that?'

'Maybe if he'd driven the truck in himself he would have thought of it. He was probably either in a tearing hurry or he was starving,' said Julia. 'Rob, did you see anything on those screens?'

'No, can't say that I did,' said Rob slowly. 'But I'm an older generation and my eyes don't automatically swivel to any screen near me, so I didn't really look at them. I did notice they were on and that there was a lot of computer type hardware on the passenger seat, but that's all.'

Julia looked out at the nearly dark forecourt and thought for a minute. 'I think you two should go home now and I'll stay here and call the cops. They'll obviously want to talk to you, Shane – you're the only one who saw what was on those screens, but I'm sure they can do that tomorrow, it's not as if it's an emergency. I do think they need to have that guy's plate number as soon as possible, though, so they can stop him if a patrol car sees him. I'll stay on until I know if they want to come over and check the footage tonight.'

On his way out Shane turned. 'Why do we

have a camera in the workshop? Is it to check that we're working?'

'God, no! But we had a couple of opportunist guys stealing expensive tools a couple of years ago - just walked in from the street and took stuff. And though we had them on the forecourt camera they cleverly carried the tools out inside their jackets, and we could only see their backs, of course, so we had no proof.' She shook her head at the memory. 'You could tell they were holding their arms across the front of their bodies in a weird way, so things wouldn't drop to the ground – it was perfectly clear. They told the cops they had just walked closer to check out a car they liked the look of.'

Half an hour later, after saving the relevant clips of footage as a file she could email, Julia spent a surprisingly long time talking to the operator at the police call centre, who demanded a lot of detail. But why? thought Julia, who wanted to go home. I'll give the cops the whole story anyway. Couldn't she just get them to call me back? She was just about to put her jacket on when a police officer knocked on the locked office door and made her jump.

'I wasn't expecting anyone to come by tonight – it's not an emergency,' said Julia when she had unlocked the door. 'I told them when I called, and I gave them the plate number and all the details.'

'I was coming back from a callout at the port and the dispatcher said to check if you were still here.' The officer listened to the story and exclaimed, 'What a shit!' and then she collected herself and added, 'Sorry, I mean what a creep.'

It made Julia laugh. 'You're welcome, the man's obviously a shit of the highest order. Did they look up the plate and get his name? He's not in our database, he just came in as a casual, paid and left. Or aren't you allowed to tell me?'

'They'll do all that at the station,' said the woman. 'I just said I'd call in on my way back and have a look at that CCTV footage. And I'll give you an incident docket with a number, so you can upload the video clips online, just follow the directions under the heading "reporting a crime" and quote the docket number. Someone will come and talk to your young mechanic, but it might be a few days – we're flat out at the moment. We'll have to get hold of those computers, of course, so we have some evidence. And I nearly forgot – your mechanic's sure this creep can't have seen him staring, is he? Just so he doesn't hide or delete evidence before someone can pay him a visit. OK, then, and don't forget to call if he turns up again before we've found him.'

'Of course,' said Julia. 'We'll disable his car in some subtle way, so he has to stay until you come and arrest him.' They both laughed and the officer left.

Driving home Julia thought of all those women at their various workplaces who had been filmed, and how they would feel when this guy appeared in court at some future date. Definitely very creepy, she thought, as she went up in the lift, and who knows, maybe I've been filmed too. The idea hadn't occurred to her before that moment, but she realised that now it would always sit in the back of her mind like an unpleasant whisper, impossible to dispel. She diverted her mind by reminding herself once again that in the morning she must brief Shane and made sure he knew how important it was that he didn't add or embellish anything. She texted him as soon she had shut the front door behind her: *Someone will come and interview you one day soon. Probably best not to put this on social media or even talk about it.* He replied instantly: *I wouldn't dare, that guy looked dangerous.*

4

The next day Rob asked Julia to show Morgan the video from the security cameras. 'We should all know what that truck looks like, you know, the logo on the doors and the guy himself, of course. Just to be on the safe side. You never know!' he added in his inimitable way of darkly hinting at things. 'We might come across him somewhere.'

Julia, who had known Rob for close on twenty years, smiled to herself at this well-established way of bringing things to her notice and said, 'Go get them and we'll do it now.'

She opened the clips she had uploaded to the police website the previous evening and waited for them to join her. 'Tell me if you want me to stop at any point. We can save still images if you need to study them.'

After watching Julia scroll through the images

for a couple of minutes Morgan said, 'Stop! Can you go back a few seconds? I think I've seen this guy before.'

Julia paused the recording where the man's face was first visible as he got out of his truck on the forecourt and then went forward frame by frame. 'Yeah, it's him, all right. He's sometimes in the Crown bar down at the fishing boat harbour. I'm often there on a Friday night with my mates and I've seen him several times. It's a guy you notice - not just his size, but he's scruffy and loud.'

'OK, I'll tell the police. And maybe we should print off that image and put it up in the lunchroom to make sure we'll all recognise him if he ever comes back. You can say we're fully booked if you like, or book him in and I'll alert the cops.' She thought for a moment. 'But I'm sure he won't come back. He would have realised as soon as he drove off that those laptops had been open all the time he was away getting his burger. I bet he'll never come near this place again.'

After lunch when Julia had just taken a call from Barb a police car drove up outside. 'Look, I'd better go,' she said quickly. 'We reported an incident yesterday and the cops just drove in.'

Ignoring Barb's question about what had

happened Julia put the phone down just as a male officer with a deep bruise on his cheekbone and raw looking abrasions along his jawline entered the office.

'Hi, I'm DC Bartholomew,' he said. 'I've come to talk to the mechanic who saw the screens in that truck yesterday. Is there somewhere he and I can sit and talk?'

Julia got up. 'I thought it would be days before you'd have time to come. You can use the lunchroom for the interview, they've all had their lunch. Come with me and we'll find Shane.'

'We're very keen to get hold of this guy before he destroys any evidence – he must have realised someone would have seen what was on those laptops.'

Saskia closed the lunchroom door around Shane and the detective and went back to the office, and half an hour later the officer returned and waited at the counter while a customer paid and left.

'He's a very observant young chap. He says he only looked at that screen for a few seconds, but he remembered how many images were on the screen and even described the colours of the walls in some of them, so very well done. Those cameras are obviously movement triggered and stop filming a few moments after a woman leaves the cubicle. But our problem now is locating the truck. The number plate's stolen, so we're doing a check on trucks of that make and model. Did you see him? You might have noticed something Shane didn't.'

He smiled, then grimaced and touched his cheekbone. He keeps forgetting that bruise, thought Julia, I wonder how many times he's done that, smiled and then felt it hurting and automatically touched it.

She shook her head. 'No, I was out picking up a parcel and they told me about him when I got back. Well, they told me a creepy guy had been in, but I didn't get the full story until the end of the day. Can't you track him by the logo on the doors – you can see the business is called Active Plumbing.'

'We tried that this morning when we saw the video clips you sent. It's not a registered business and there's no trace of it anywhere. So far we haven't found anyone in the trade who's heard of Active Plumbing, so we're up against a dead end there. But plenty of traffic cameras to help us check where he went from here.' Bartholomew frowned. 'Either he isn't a plumber at all, and he just uses the name as a ruse to get access to toilets and put in cameras, or perhaps he's a one man band and just calls himself Active Plumbing. We tried social media too, but that name isn't anywhere. One of your mechanics told me he's seen him a few times down at the Crown on a Friday night, so we'll check that out now we have his face from your CCTV.'

He was turning to leave when Julia thought of something. 'Hey, listen – have you come across this before? I mean cameras in toilets?'

'Not personally, but of course I know it happens – toilets and women's changing rooms, public swimming pools. Why?'

'Why do you think they do it? I mean specifically toilets. It isn't as if anyone gets undressed in public restrooms, is it?' She looked carefully at him to see if he found her question strange, but he was a male and maybe he would be able to explain it. 'It's not as if they'd see a lot – it just seems weird. Or do they get turned on by watching women sitting on the toilet? It seems so odd.'

'I've no idea - I don't get it either,' Bartholomew grinned and touched his bruised cheekbone again. 'Did Shane tell you about the camera angles?'

'No – what about the angles?'

'From behind, to one side and from below – like he's mounted a tiny camera in the rear corner, close to the floor looking up, Shane said. So, he'd have pretty invasive views as women were in the process of sitting down. And he must have concealed the cameras, however small, as something else – devious and clever.'

He shook his head in disgust and Julia studied

him for a moment then made an impulsive decision and said, 'Just wait a moment, will you? I'll be right back.'

She left him standing there, went back to the lunchroom and returned with a small tube in her hand. 'Here, put some of this on your bruise, I can see it hurts when you smile. This will help and it's harmless. Where you in a fight?'

Taken aback he automatically took the tube she held out and said casually, 'A difference of opinion with a drunk yesterday. It happens.'

'Use it!' said Julia. 'It's just arnica in the form of an ointment. We always have it in the first aid cabinet, it helps with bruises and dulls the pain – we have frequent minor injuries here, so we're well stocked up with first aid materials.' She watched him rub a little on the bruise and accepted the tube back. 'And we'll tell you if we ever see that pervert again.'

When Bartholomew left she stood there for a moment with the tube of ointment in her hand, deep in thought. She pictured a man who parked a truck with a logo on the door outside some big workplace and entered with a bag of plumber's tools in his hand, maybe wearing a high-viz vest. Would he casually sign a visitors' register and say he'd been called to check the ladies' toilets? Did he perhaps have a sign with him to put on the door saying that repairs were underway and to use another restroom, maybe one of those fold-out signs you put on the floor? Walking back to the lunchroom with the tube of arnica she elaborated on that thought and tried to imagine how the images got to his laptops. Presumably it involved a link via his phone, but she didn't know enough about it and would do some research that evening because a technical mystery of any kind would haunt her if she didn't find the answer.

5

_T_he second text from Stuart a week after the first was nasty. She had picked up the phone from her bedside table when it pinged, and now she stood with the phone in her hand and tried to decide what to do. The message was typical of him and read, *I see you date guys young enough to be your son now. Does it make you feel younger? I think we need to talk about this, my treasure.*

Why did he feel a need to start taunting her again after a silence of a year and half since the serious harassment ended? He had pursued her for a long time after she broke up with him, and very nearly turned into a stalker. At one stage she had even avoided going out at night because he seemed to turn up at the same places far more regularly than she would have expected, particularly seeing that she had changed her habits and avoid going to the places they had frequented together. It was only after she bought a new phone that they stopped coinciding at various restaurants and bars, and only then had she thought of the possibility that he had put a tracking app on her old phone.

Looking back on their relationship now, she could see the pattern that had emerged over time, the slow changes that hadn't been apparent at the start. How Stuart's behaviour had become more controlling and the passive aggressive comments became more frequent as time went on. And his aggression, which was always verbal and never physical, became less passive and more open and developed into sessions of blame, recriminations and accusations of various kind.

She only realised in retrospect that he might have been using the aggression as a tool to manipulate her, make her feel worthless and unsure of herself. The final straw that made her act on her developing unhappiness was one evening when he shouted at her that she was useless, a complete failure and only good to look at, when she'd forgotten something he had asked her to pick up on her way home from work. She had stood up to him, and after a furious confrontation she told him to get out that very moment or she would call the police and get a trespass order against him. She had remained standing in the middle of the living room with her phone in her hand and the front door wide open until he had packed a small bag and left, not prepared to take any chances. She texted him the moment he left and said to make an appointment when he was coming to pick up the rest of his things, as she wanted to have another person present. To avoid worrying Barb she hadn't asked Anthony to be her bodyguard, so instead she asked Rob to be there.

'It's not that I think he's going to be violent,' she said. 'You won't have to fight him or anything, he's never been violent. I just want to avoid being stood over and shouted at again.'

But it didn't end there. For some time after he had picked up his belongings, Stuart had persisted in turning up on her doorstep as if he actually believed that they were still in a relationship, and she had a peephole installed in the door so she could avoid opening it when he was outside. He acted as if he still had a right to claim her attention and to touch her when they met out, and that had been the hardest thing to stop until she got her new phone and those accidental-on- purpose meetings stopped. She engaged a male friend to act as if he was a new boyfriend, to go on dates that looked romantic but weren't, and it had worked. Stuart stepped back and abandon his pursuit. She was certain that his persistence had nothing to do with love and everything to do with his fury at having been thrown out, dismissed with instant effect. His overwhelming self-pride made it impossible for him to understand that a woman might simply get tired of his corrosive personality.

After a few minutes contemplating his message, she put the phone down and finished getting dressed. She wouldn't respond to that text either and should probably block him. Getting into any kind of discussion with him was out of the question. It made her tired just to think of coming up against his unshakeable belief that he should win every argument. And then she did it straight away, picked up the phone again and blocked him. They had nothing in common now, there was absolutely no possibility that they would meet for a conversation, as he suggested.

The next few days she was busy, and it wasn't until the following weekend that she suddenly thought of him again when she was getting ready to go to the international food fair at the stadium with a group of friends, something she and Stuart had done together the two years they were together. To feel that this thought was like a premonition was ridiculous, and she told herself that she was just being overly aware of him at the moment. If she hadn't got those messages from Stuart just recently she would never have thought of the food fair as a place where something embarrassing might happen. She couldn't change everything in her life simply to avoid meeting him, however unpleasant it would probably be if the last time they had met was anything to go by. She must be allowed to carry on her life the way she wanted to, and at least there would be no more messages now.

The annual food fair was a huge and very popular event, always fun with dozens of stalls manned by local businesses and some from further away, food from various ethnic groups to sample and to buy, and nearly always friends to catch up with, met accidentally at one stall or another. As arranged Greta and her partner Rocky swung by her apartment to pick her up, then parked on a side street and waited by gate H for the second couple to arrive, standing quietly talking and watching people go by.

Then someone touched Julia's shoulder and before she even heard his voice she knew from the expression on Greta's face that it was Stuart; she had always disliked him and had never been able to conceal her opinion.

'Hello, my treasure,' said Stuart and pulled her close to his side with an arm over her shoulders. 'How are you? Still running around with that schoolboy or are you ready to come back to me now?'

Julia swung fast out of his hold and took a step to one side, outraged at this arrogant display of entitlement. 'Stuart,' she said and tried to keep her voice even and not reveal how furious she was, which would only feed into his egotistical mind. 'I'm not running around with schoolboys. The friend you sent that ridiculous text message about is just a young chap who wanted some of advice about changing his job and training as a mechanic, the son of a customer. Not that it's any business of yours, but it's interesting that seeing me with him seems to have got on your nerves.'

She knew that dig would get to him, that she should probably not have said it, and now there would be some kind of payback, but she couldn't resist.

'You naughty wench!' said Stewart, and gave her a look that she knew well, a signal that this wasn't over because he hadn't yet won, and he would continue goading her until he felt he had thoroughly trounced her.

Just then, with Greta's face clearly displaying her irritated impatience and Rocky shifting from one foot to the other ready to intervene, their friends arrived, and as luck would have it one of them was somebody Stuart obviously had an issue with. Julia sensed his displeasure and ignored his goodbye, turned to the others and didn't watch him walk away. As their group walked into the stadium Greta took Julia's arm and said quietly, 'You're not seeing him again are you? What was that schoolboy comment really about?'

'No of course I'm not seeing him again, I'd never have anything more to do with him if I could help it. He couldn't resist a taunt the other day after he saw me out with a young guy who asked me out for a drink, so he sent me a text message that I didn't reply to. I wish he'd give up - I don't think he wants to get together again. It's just that he resents that I was the one who broke it off. He can't accept that anyone else has the right to change the status of anything. It should be his prerogative - he should be the boss and in charge of everything.'

'He's got an inflated sense of self entitlement,' said Greta decisively. 'He always did, and I must say that I, and most people who know you, never understood why you got together with him in the first place. He's not in your class, Julia.'

'It was a bit silly,' said Julia reluctantly. 'I've made a couple of mistakes with men in my life, but that one was the worst by far.'

The rest of the afternoon was spent moving through the crowd, buying products, getting separated and then finding each other again, until by five o'clock they were all exhausted and left, agreeing to meet at Julia's apartment for a drink. The evening turned into an impromptu meal with what she had in the fridge added to by their various purchases from the food fair and continued to after midnight. After drawn-out and noisy goodbyes Julia tidied the kitchen and started the dishwasher, and once again her thoughts reverted to how infuriating Stuart's behaviour was and wondered if there was anything she could do to stop him. Why she had got to the age she had without finding someone who truly understood her, someone she could trust and love deeply? Was there something in her personality that put the right kind of men off? Was she perhaps too bossy, too used to running a business, telling people what to do, or too practical and organised for men of the right kind to feel attracted to? Or was it just bad luck and timing? Perhaps one day someone would turn up in her life and she would look at him and think, 'There he is – finally!' Then she laughed at herself for being a romantic fool at her age, turned the lights off and went to bed.

6

One day not long after the food fair incident, Rob came into the office and said urgently, 'Julia, come with me for a moment, will you?' and led the way back to the workshop.

'Stand here, right in the corner.' He pointed to the furthest corner from the office. 'See that red car on the far side of the street, just past the green station wagon?'

Julia looked where he pointed and saw an old red Toyota but failed to understand why he had pointed it out. 'And? What about it?'

'He's been there twice already in the last few days, arrives around lunch time and stays there for an hour or two and then he drives away. Doesn't get out.'

He looked expectantly at her, and she looked silently back. There was something going on in that cunning, grey head, but she had no idea what it was. 'Do you think he's going to rob us? Do you know who it is?'

'We think it's a stalker.'

Julia burst out laughing. 'Really? Why would you think that – and who is he stalking? Have you guys eaten magic mushrooms or something?'

Rob led her back to the office and the other mechanics followed. Leaning on the counter Rob said, 'Now listen to this and stop joking! Shane thought it might be the creepy guy – he got worried he's found out we reported him, but it's not him. We think it's someone who's watching you. You can try and laugh it off if you like, but you know we're not the kind of guys who panic about things. And this is weird.'

'You guys have gone mad,' said Julia. 'Whoever's in that car can't even see this end of the building, and I hardly ever go outside during the day, so they'll never see me. Why would someone park there if they were after watching me? They'd be parking a lot closer. They're probably stalking one of you.'

Shane cleared his throat. 'I walked around the block at lunchtime yesterday carrying my phone in my hand – you know, like I was watching something on the screen, and I've got a photo of him. Took it as I walked past – he was looking in this direction and not at me. And it's not the creepy guy, it's someone I've never seen before.'

'Show me!' Julia took the phone Shane held

out and looked at the profile of the man taken through the side window, slightly blurry but clear enough to see he was a good looking middle-aged man with a buzz cut. 'Nope, I've never seen him before either. Maybe he's spying on someone who works in MacDonald's – that's closer than our place.'

Shane protested instantly. 'No! He's not looking at MacDonalds – look at the photo again. He was parked nearly exactly where he is today, so imagine where I was when I took the photo and check the angle of his head. He's definitely looking towards this place. I saw him first on Friday last week – he was a bit closer then.'

'Let's all go back to work,' said Julia briskly. 'We've got no real reason to think he's a stalker, but I could go down and ask what he's doing, I suppose. That would probably solve the problem – or we could just ignore him.'

'Don't you do any such thing!' Morgan's exclamation was forceful, and Julia realised they were genuinely worried, though she couldn't for the life of her imagine why, when there was no real reason to think the man in the car really was a stalker. But seeing the expression on Morgan's face she realised she must calm them down and promise to obey, so she laughed and said mockingly, 'OK – thanks for worrying about me. I promise not to go and talk to that man.'

'Good,' said Rob. 'I can tell you think we're

crazy, but we see the way customers, guys, look at you. We hear how they sound when they talk to you too – you're a very beautiful woman and men try to chat you up. We sometimes comment on it and keep an eye on people, so you won't be subjected to a load of crap from random guys.'

'Really? I had no idea - but thank you, though I'm sure it not necessary.'

'That cop,' said Morgan. 'The one who came to talk to Shane.'

This was going too far, and she had to stop it. 'Bartholomew? You're kidding, he was as nice and polite as you could wish for.'

'You didn't see the way he looked at your backside when he followed you to the lunchroom. Not that I think he'd do or say anything, but it's typical of how men look at you. Both Rob and I noticed. Just keep your eyes open when you go home in case this fellow follows you.'

They all trooped back out to the workshop and left Julia wondering if there was something they hadn't told her. She had never had them act protective before, and none of them had ever before mentioned her looks or voiced any concern about male customers. She was well aware of the interest men showed in her, but it had been part of her life since her teens and she paid little attention. Apart from Ashton, no customer had been more than mildly flirty, though sometimes when she was out men would approach her with invitations varying from polite offers of a drink to more blatant sexual suggestions.

Late afternoon she went back to the far corner of the workshop to look down the street and the car was gone. Rob saw her checking and came over. 'He left not long after we talked to you. We'll watch out from now on in case he comes back again.'

7

*J*ulia had no idea what hit her; all she knew was that something crashed into her from the side. She fell hard and nearly blacked out for a moment, opened her eyes and looked into the terrified face of a little boy on the verge of tears.

'I'm so sorry! It's my fault! Are you all right? Let me help you up.' His frantic voice was overtaken by another, and a woman pushed him roughly to one side and bent over Julia. 'You'd best lie still – you've had a terrible blow to the head, I saw your head hit the paving. I've called for an ambulance.'

Julia stayed where she was, feeling slightly ridiculous and reluctant to meet anyone's eyes. What an embarrassing thing to happen, she thought, closed her eyes and listened to the various exclamations around her; a man agreeing with the bossy woman that one should never take head injuries lightly, and someone asking the woman if they should help Julia sit up. The answer was an uncompromising no – they were not going help Julia up until the ambulance arrived. After a few moments she opened her eyes and said to nobody in particular, 'My satchel? Where is it?'

'Right here,' said the boy, who was now sitting on the sidewalk beside her. 'I've got it. I thought someone might nick it.'

She had to smile despite the intense pain in her head. There he was, probably only eight or nine, sitting cross-legged beside her left shoulder with her satchel on one side and his school backpack on the other.

'Don't look so worried,' she said quietly and tried to smile at his concerned face. 'Accidents happen. Were you on a scooter?'

'Yeah, and I was going too fast, I know I was - I'm so sorry - and then you turned and kind of changed direction just as I was passing you and ..'

He was near tears still, upset and talking very fast. Julia made an effort to sound comforting. 'Don't worry, I'm sure I'll just have a headache for a couple of days and a lump on my head. I might even get a day or two off if I play this right.'

She gestured for him to bend closer and said, as if she was telling him a secret, 'If I wasn't so scared of that bossy woman I'd get up right now. What's your name?'

'Seb. Well, it's really Sebastian, but nobody calls me that apart from my mother sometimes, even my godfather doesn't – I'm named after him. My surname's McLeod. Are you going to sue me?'

'Of course not! Why on earth would I do that?'

'They always do on TV – I thought you might want to.' He frowned. 'I think I deserve to be sued.'

'Nonsense,' said Julia and supressed a groan of pain to avoid alarming this lovely kid. 'It was just one of those things. I'm going to close my eyes now, because I'm right in line with the reflections off that car.'

She didn't point, but the boy looked around and she saw him measure the angle and decide which car it was, then he shuffled along on his bottom until his shadow fell over her face. 'Is that better?'

'You know what?' said Julia, the way her nephew always said it with the emphasis on *what*. 'You're an amazing boy, Seb, very kind and clever. I couldn't have been knocked over by anyone nicer. You should tell your parents I said that – in case they get angry with you.'

'I might,' said Seb doubtfully, and the frown

was back. 'Dad might understand, but my mum will be cross. What's your name?'

'Julia Tallboy,' she just had time to say and then a paramedic was crouching on her other side and when she next looked to her left, Sebastian had gone.

Keeping her in hospital overnight seemed to Julia like erring on the side of over-caution, but the ED doctor persuaded her not to go home.

'Just one night,' she said. 'I never feel happy about people going home with a concussion if they live alone. I'll put it in your notes that I want whoever's on tomorrow morning to do another couple of reflex tests before they discharge you.'

Issued with a hospital gown, Julia sat in a bed in a small room where two beds were empty and one was occupied by a girl with two broken legs, one suspended in traction.

'Very unusual,' said the nurse who settled Julia in. 'I can't remember when we last had two empty beds in this ward. We had to squeeze in extra beds everywhere during the epidemic. This room used to be a two-bed room, but we seem to mostly be full even now when Covid's died down. And our young friend over there is Linda, who had a bad fall when skateboarding.'

'Is it nice to sometimes have the room to

yourself?' said Julia to her room-mate when the nurse had left. 'I suppose it's great when you have visitors – you can make as much noise as you like.'

'I don't get many visitors - well, not any now,' said Linda without any visible sign of self-pity. 'I did have a few at first, friends from the polytechnic. It's my first year and I haven't really had time to make many friends.'

Julia leaned back against the pillows and closed her eyes for a moment, trying to decide if it would be better not to ask any further questions, but the thought of this lonely girl lying there helpless after she herself had returned to her flat was too sad to contemplate. How lonely she must feel.

'Does your family live far away?'

'My parents work of the UN – they're both nurses, they're in Bangladesh. They've been there for six months. It's a two-year thing and they might roll over their contract for another two years. They say they finally feel they're doing something truly worthwhile.'

'What do you need? I mean, books, fruit? Anything I can bring after they let me go home tomorrow?'

'My friends from the student hostel brought my laptop, so I can watch things and read – and study, and I had my phone with me when I got hit but luckily it wasn't smashed. It's just frustrating that I can't sit up properly, just kind of sit halfway like this.' She made a disgusted face. 'And I hate not being able to go to the toilet – I've been here for a while now and I'm still not used to it.'

Julia gave her a wry smile across the room. 'I can imagine! I was hit by a little boy on a scooter and knocked myself stupid when I crashed to the ground. Did someone on a skateboard hit you?'

'No, I was in a half pipe, and I'd just got a lot of air at the vert ramp and turned to drop back in, and someone crashed into me. I cartwheeled right down to the bottom of the pipe.'

Julia started to laugh and winced at the pain on the side of her head. 'Translation, please! I haven't the slightest idea what you just told me.'

Linda grinned across the room and her face transformed into that of a mischievous child. 'That was a bit evil, it's skateboarding talk. Sorry! What I should have said was that I went zooming down from the edge at the top of the slope, up the other side and way up into the air – where I turned. And as I was dropping back down, just about to touch down a meter or so from the lip, someone came flying up at an angle and we collided.'

'Oh, my God, that must have hurt! And what happened to the other person – did he get hurt?'

Linda smiled again, probably at her assumption that the other skateboarder was male. 'Nearly totally unhurt – she had a few grazes and a broken wrist. But she came to see me a couple of times the first week, and she brought flowers and chocolates. Her name's Bella. But it wasn't her fault, it was just bad timing. She's still leaning to judge speed and distance and keep an eye out at the same time.'

8

A couple of hours later, after Julia had slept for an hour, she was offered dinner at the surprisingly early hour of half past five.

'It's normal here,' Linda told her when the large stainless steel trolley had moved on. 'They start at this end of the ward and apparently the people down the other end don't get theirs until more than half an hour later. Then they want to pick up all plates and things before the next shift comes on at seven.'

Julia had turned down the offer of dinner but accepted a cup of coffee and an apple and settled down to read a book on the Kindle app on her phone. The painkillers had kicked in and muted the pain in her head, and she was feeling relatively normal.

When someone said her name she looked up

and there was Sebastian in the doorway and behind him a woman who was obviously his mother; the likeness was so startling it made Julia smile. They had the same dark brown hair and intensely blue eyes, and the same deeply curving smile.

'We've come to see how you are,' said Sebastian and off-loaded a large box of chocolates and a bunch of flowers on the foot of Julia's bed. 'And I'm supposed to apologise and say I've learnt my lesson.'

'Oh, what lovely flowers, and chocolates too - thank you Seb! And no more apologies, please, we've done that bit already, so now we can just have a chat. And you'll have to introduce me to your mother.'

'Mum, this is Julia -and this is my mum whose name is Prissy. But she's not – not prissy, I mean. That's my dad's joke, it's not very funny. I should have said mum's name is Pricilla, but nobody ever calls her that.'

Sebastian's mother was clearly embarrassed. 'I'm so sorry this happened, but it will be a lesson for him to be more careful in future. I was pleased he remembered your full name, or we'd never have found you. How badly hurt are you?'

'Practically unhurt,' said Julia and smiled at Sebastian. 'If Seb and I hadn't been so scared of the bossy lady, who took charge at the scene, I'd have got up and walked away. It's only a lump on my head and a headache. They're being overly cautious, I think. Let's agree right now, Seb – it was half my fault for changing direction so abruptly without looking, I could have knocked some old, frail person over! And the other half is your fault for going so fast. Which half of the blame do you want? The lump or the headache?'

Sebastian giggled and his mother smiled. 'You're being very kind! Seb's been full of self-blame.'

'Seb,' said Julia, who had noticed his eyes drifting back to the bed on the other side of the room more than once, probably fascinated by Linda's leg held high in the air by the traction wires attached to it. 'Could you please figure out how to open that box of chocolates, so you can take it across to poor Linda and give her a few. She's stuck in her bed as you can see, and she doesn't have any visitors.'

Seb didn't need to be told twice; he picked up the box and ripped the cellophane open as he walked across the room, and Julia turned back to Prissy.

'Don't be cross with him or punish him, please. He was such a star at the scene, you should be very proud of him. He looked after me and took charge of my bag in case someone tried to take it. He sat right beside my shoulder for quarter of an hour and moved so the sun wouldn't be in my eyes.'

Julia continued to talk to Prissy, but now and then she glanced across the room. Seb was now perched on the edge of Linda's bed, and with their heads close together, one dark and one blond, they were reading the back of the box and identifying which flavour was which and discussing which were their favourites.

Julia said quietly, 'Look at him now, cheering up that poor girl with her broken legs, seriously damaged. She has no family locally, her parents are working overseas, and this isn't her hometown. I'll have to do something about it, or she'll be stuck here for weeks. The student hostel probably won't have her back until she's properly mobile again.'

'What will you do?' Prissy looked part surprised, and part fascinated. 'I mean, what *could* you do?'

'Oh, this and that - just practical things. Like find out what's happened to her hostel room and her belongings, how long until she's out of traction, where will she go when she's a bit mobile. I can't let her lie here for weeks like abandoned luggage with two legs in casts.'

'Really? You would make yourself responsible for her?'

'Someone should,' said Julia and watched Linda explain how the traction worked to Seb, who listened, totally absorbed. 'I can organise it, provided she'll let me.'

Amazing woman. Julia nearly jumped. What was that? A voice in her head, like the dim, distant sound of someone talking far away. She shook her head and dismissed it. Someone must have spoken in the corridor, and the muted words had somehow shifted so they sounded as if they were inside her head.

'Do you need any help?' asked Prissy now. 'I'd like to do something for you.'

'God no, there's nothing wrong with me. I'll go home tomorrow morning and change my clothes and go back to work. I called in while I was waiting in ED and told them I wouldn't be in for the rest of today. The less fuss the better.'

Prissy said apologetically, 'Sorry, I didn't mean what could I do for you, though I would do whatever you need, but you seem totally organised. I meant could I help you get things organised for this girl? Perhaps when you know a bit more you could delegate a few things to me.'

Julia thought for a moment. How would this work? 'Let's exchange phone numbers,' she said finally, having found no immediate answers. 'I'll call you when I've found out more. I'll have to talk to her and then to the staff here and at her hostel and probably her tutors too, it's kind of layered, I'll start on it this week, but I might leave talking to Linda until I know exactly what I can offer her.'

'OK,' said Prissy and got her phone out. 'Put

your number in my phone and I'll text you, so you have mine. I'm afraid we must go now. I've got to get Seb fed and check that he does his homework and then prepare some snacks before my book club friends arrive at eight tonight. My husband's away on a job in Nelson this week, so I have to be both parents rolled into one.'

When they had left Julia closed her eyes, leaned back against the pillow and tried to make sense of that comment she thought she had heard. Not only had the voice been oddly impersonal, more like a digital voice, but she had experienced a brief mist of colour in front of her eyes, a pale green like diluted watercolour. It had gone as quickly as it appeared, but now she was beginning to wonder if something was wrong with her vision, that the concussion had somehow damaged her more than she had thought. But after considering this for a couple of minutes she opened her eyes again, looked across at Linda who was holding up the box of chocolates clearly wondering how to get it back to Julia's side, and laughed. Becoming too aware of little changes and worrying about the concussion would do her no good.

'You could try throwing it,' she said to Linda, who started to laugh and held the box up above her head as if she was really going to throw it. 'Or just pick out one or two and toss them across. I like the ones without soft fillings if there are any left.'

'Plenty of solid chocolate ones left. Sebastian ate most of the soft centre ones. I bet he'll be sick in the car on the way home, and it would serve him right, I told him not to be so greedy.'

She picked up three chocolates and threw them one by one in a beautiful arc across the room, until they were all on Julia's bed. She unwrapped one and popped it in her mouth and thought how good it had been to see Linda interacting with Sebastian. The fact that the girl of her age could get such pleasure out of talking to a little boy told her something about Linda's character, and she knew she must definitely do something about her future.

9

*A*fter only three dates with Ashton Julia knew that she had made a mistake when she agreed to go out with him. They had nothing in common apart from physical attraction, but Ashton now imagined himself deeply in love with her. She didn't think his assertion of real love was probable, but whether it was or not was immaterial. She couldn't let this go any further for several reasons. Their interests and tastes were poles apart even down to things like preferred foods and places to meet. Their conversations had become exercises in patience for Julia, as she listened to Ashton telling her things about his day and his interests, while she tried to think of how to respond or how to change the subject to something that even vaguely interested her without being boring for him.

His interests were limited, and his main topics of conversation revolved around sports, mainly rugby league and basketball, what his workmates and customers had said that day, and detailed stories about fishing trips with his brother. A recurring theme was the long weekend coming up in a month and he had all sorts of ideas for things that they could do together, but none appealed to Julia. She wasn't keen on fishing trips in weather that would be really cold by then and going to stay in a motel simply to be somewhere else, presumably with the intention of spending a long weekend in bed, didn't entice her however attractive she found Ashton.

Julia's ideas of interesting holidays consisted of two extremes, and she knew without voicing them that neither would appeal to Ashton. She loved tramping alone in national parks, or if she took someone with her it must be someone who shared her interest in native birds and trees. Her other favourite holiday consisted of going to another city, which one was immaterial, to visit art exhibitions, have wonderful meals in fancy restaurants and maybe go to a musical, things she rarely did in her hometown. She had never worked out why she hardly ever did those things in her daily non-holiday life, where she mostly did nothing more ambitious than meet friends for coffee or a drink or spend time with Barb's family, but that's how it was. She had developed a habit of saving up her personal interests and enthusiasms for a few days of concentrated art and food experiences in some other location, and once a year a four or five-day tramp in a national park, quite happy to do it on her own. Her sisters thought her solitary breaks of self-indulgence were odd and often asked why she didn't take someone with her for company. There was no answer that would satisfy them, so Julia usually said she was just different and liked being alone.

But now she knew the Ashton affair must end before it went any further, before he began to believe they were a couple with a future. If she let it carry on he would feel worse when she broke it off than at this early stage, and the last thing she wanted to do was hurt him. She asked for them to meet over a drink straight after work one night and told him that she would not be seeing him anymore. She emphasised that he was a lovely guy, and she was very fond of him, but she wasn't in love with him and never would be. He didn't take it well and tried to convince her that if they continued seeing each other something would develop between them, something meaningful and lasting. He even said that he didn't care if she didn't love him so long as they stayed together. They parted after an hour and Julia walked back to her car, her feelings a mixture of guilt and relief.

. . .

Three days later, after several text messages from Ashton which had been difficult to respond to without hurting him, she watched a motorbike park outside her office. As the rider pulled his helmet off and walked towards her she wondered why they had so few clients with motorbikes. Probably they go the specialist garages, she thought, but I'm sure the guys here would love a change from cars and vans.

'Hi,' he said. 'I'm Angus, Ashton's older brother.'

Various ideas about why he was there appeared in Julia's mind, none of them pleasant, but all she said was, 'Hi Angus,' and waited. She could see that he was hesitating, not quite sure how to start.

'This is a bit embarrassing,' he said finally and looked slightly to the left of her, as if he found it hard to meet her eyes. 'I know this seems weird, but I've come to talk about Ashton - and let me say right away that he doesn't know I'm here, and I don't want him to know. He gave me your phone number and I promised to call you. But he's devastated. I've never seen him like this in my life. He says he'll do anything to get you to stay with him, and he can't understand why you said it's over and won't try for it to grow into something lasting.'

Julia tried to think of a way to explain why she had broken it off without being insulting, but it was hard to think of anything but the truth or maybe a softened version of the truth. She obviously couldn't say that one of the reasons, or perhaps the main reason, for the break-up was that they had nothing in common and his conversation bored her.

'It's not because I don't like him,' she said slowly. 'He's a lovely guy, and he deserves better then someone who doesn't really love him – which I don't. I know he says he doesn't care that I'm a lot older than he is, and he might think that's my reason, but that's not why I broke it off. We really have very little in common, and I think it's better to say it's over at this early stage than to continue and make it more complicated later on.'

Angus looked hard at her, and she could see that he was trying to decide if she was being honest or if there was something else that had caused her to tell Ashton she wouldn't see him again.

'Is that it?' he asked finally. 'Just that you don't think it's ever going to really turn into love for you? So, it's not that he's done something wrong, something that upset you? He's really worried it's something he did or said.'

Julia smiled and tried to make what she was going to say sound casual but honest. 'Oh no, your brother is a lovely, kind guy, but I don't love him. And I never pretended I did. I like his company and who could resist someone so good looking? But I wasn't falling in love with him, and I won't be. I'm at fault here for giving in to temptation – feeling flattered that he wanted to go out with me and giving in when he kept asking. I should never have let it start, and I feel guilty now that I did. If I continued this relationship I'd feel as if I was using him, and he might be even more reluctant to accept a break-up at some stage in the future. Which would inevitably happen because this can never become a lasting relationship apart from on a friendship level.'

'OK, I get it. But how I'm going to get Ashton to accept that's all it is? That it's over and that you have a good reason. It's going to be very hard for him to accept that it's only because you're never going to fall in love with him. He's quite convinced that if you saw him a few more times, or at least once or twice, you would understand that because he loves *you*, you would also come to love him. That's what he said last night when he told me what he was so upset about.'

Guilt and regret swamped Julia's mind and made her voice sound sadder than she had intended. 'I'm sorry Angus, but there's nothing I can do about it.' She watched his face for a moment and finally found a way to cope with this that didn't insult Ashton, something Angus would be able to convey convincingly. 'I *did* think I would fall in love with him when I first said I'd go out with him. Because, as I said, he is so charming and good looking and so kind, and I thought I would inevitably fall in love. But I didn't - and I know I won't. Continuing having an affair with him when I know this – I just can't, it would be cruel, and it would lead to nothing. Do you think you can explain that to him?'

Using a lie to phrase this explanation to sound acceptable went against the grain, but it was necessary. She had never expected to fall in love with him even at the outset, but she hoped saying she had imagined that she might fall in love him made it sound more reasonable.

For the first time since he entered Angus smiled and said quietly, 'I'm sure I can get him to see that. Maybe not immediately, but over time. I've always been able to help him deal with things. He's eight years younger than I am, and he always comes to me when he needs advice. And I totally believe what you say - I think you're very sensible. To continue this affair would be unkind to Ashton if you don't have strong feelings for him. And I'll tell him it's not because of anything he did or said, it's just the way it is.'

'Thank you, Angus,' said Julia with a heartfelt sigh. 'He's very lucky to have a brother like you.'

'There's only one thing.' Angus paused and looked as if he was unsure of how his next comment would be received. 'He wants you to meet him one last time, and he told me he understands it might be the last time. He just wants to talk to you once more over a drink or a meal, to say goodbye properly, and he's promised me he won't make a fuss in public. Would you do that?'

Julia quickly tried to imagine what this final drink or meal might turn into, public embarrassment, raised voices or even tears. 'Only if you can assure me that you think he won't make a scene in a public place because that would be such a bad end to this brief affair, for him and for me.'

'I don't think he will,' said Angus with a slight frown. 'I know he's immature and not very experienced, but he's not the kind of guy to lose it in public. And he knows that if you agree to meet him, you're doing him a favour. Will you do it?'

Julia thought only for a moment before she made up her mind. She would have to be very careful with what she said and how she said it to avoid embarrassment, but it was a simple request, and she couldn't refuse. 'OK, tell him I'll meet him tonight at the French Bistro and we can have a casual meal or bar food and a drink. Tell him I'll be there at seven.'

Angus turned to go, but he stopped just by the door and turned to face her. 'He told me you're an amazing woman and I quite agree. I didn't understand why he was so desperate to continue this, but now that I've met you I think I do.'

Julia slowly shook her head and said, 'You're a such good brother, Angus. He's lucky to have you in his life. Thank you!'

And with that Angus left, put his helmet on as he walked back on his bike and rode away, leaving Julia wondering with some trepidation how that evening's date would turn out.

At ten to seven that night Julia sat down at a small table in the French Bistro where she had arrived early with the intention of making sure they would get a table that wasn't right next to anyone else, just in case this final meeting with Ashton became fraught with emotion. She had her lines rehearsed because she knew it would be important to express herself exactly right. Her main objective was to avoid making Ashton feel silly or dismissed or not good enough. She couldn't possibly tell him the unvarnished truth, that apart from mutual physical attraction they had nothing in common and he bored her, which would be dismissive and insulting. So, the right words and tone of voice were hugely important. She doubted that he would understand how significant this lack of common interests and topics of conversation was to her. That they couldn't discuss books because he didn't read books, that they didn't like the same films, and that the things he watched on TV were invariably things she would never waste an hour on. He didn't follow politics or any general news, had never played a board game like Scrabble, had no interest in art and thought musicals sounded boring. And if she continued to see him and went to bed with him a second time and maybe a third, she would be using him for her own pleasure, which would make her feel bad about herself.

She watched him enter and look around, and his face didn't light up as it usually did when he saw her, so she knew his brother had probably managed to convince him that their affair was over. Regret that she had allowed this to start at all filled her with guilt, and she could only hope that Angus had put her reasons in a way that didn't make Ashton feel belittled.

'Hi,' he said when he arrived at her table. He sat down and looked silently at her, waiting for her to start the conversation. For the first time in her life Julia found it hard to think of a single thing to say, but something had to be said; they couldn't sit there in silence staring at each other.

'Let's order some bar food and a drink,' she said and tried to sound normal. 'I think everything is easier to talk about, even very difficult things, over a glass of wine or a beer.

Let's see if we can have a quiet talk and part as friends.'

What followed was a mixture of emotions barely held in check on Ashtons part, and a concerted effort on Julia's part to keep her voice even, to give him the occasional smile and not let him dwell on the idea that if they continued to see each other she might fall in love with him. It was hard to convey to him that sometimes you know that you will never fall in love with someone however nice they are, and however much you want it to happen, and she could only hope that as he grew up a bit more he would realise that she had been right.

Gradually he seemed less tense, and she was grateful there had been no open outbreak of emotion. They both made an effort to end the meal in control of their feelings and managed to carry on a reasonably normal conversation. When they got up to leave Julia heard a comment about her and Ashton and swung around to see who was speaking. The only person looking at her was Milton Parker who was seated at a table on the far side of the room with a group of people, but he was too far away for her to have heard anything he might have said.

After an awkward parting from Ashton Julia walked slowly back to her car thinking of the comment she thought she had just heard, and how her mind had experienced a fleeting impression of muted red, as if a drift of coloured smoke had swept in front of her eyes. She felt a flash of fear, a moment of near panic, and wondered how these things were connected, and why they happened. These strange things that had only been happening since her concussion; hearing comments inside her head as if spoken by disembodied voices, and the strange brief sensations of colour that accompanied those comments. The way she was certain that what she heard inside her head were really the thoughts of others. Was this head injury more serious than she had thought? Would it get worse and worse, would she see things that weren't there, experience hallucinations? She tried to dismiss the thought that she might be losing her mind, but though she pushed the idea to one side and tried to ignore it, she knew the worry wouldn't go away. Somehow she must work it out, find an explanation reasonable enough to accept.

11

Julia always enjoyed dinner at Barb's house, perhaps mainly because of the total contrast to her own life in her apartment where everything had a place, where no bundles of clean washing waited on an armchair to be folded, and the kitchen was always tidy. At Julia's place the kitchen bench was cleared and wiped straight after each meal, and she made the bed after getting dressed each morning, even though nobody apart from she herself would see it. Barb's house was the extreme opposite where untidiness and minor chaos reigned unresolved and seemingly unnoticed by either parent, where kids' toys and discarded sneakers and jerseys littered the living room, and the kitchen always seemed to be either ready for a culinary feast or the end result of one that had just been consumed.

This evening was no exception and Julia opened the front door to hear a shriek of fury from her niece Debbie, who at six already had the pitch and volume of an opera soprano, accompanied by gales of laughter from her brother James. She walked into the living room where her entry disrupted the bedlam with both children rushing at her and hugging her around the waist and talking at the same time.

'Hang on, you little savages,' said Anthony and tried to prise James' arms from Julia's waist. 'Let the poor woman catch her breath, you're like an assault troop, you two.'

'Hi kids,' said Julia, brushed Anthony aside and put her arms around both children. 'How are you, my quiet little darlings? I came in the door and the peace and calm here was just so restful after a hard day at work, like heaven.'

The children let go of her and giggled, Anthony went off to get her a glass of wine and Debbie said hesitantly, 'Was that sarcasm, Julia?'

'What an impressive word! Where did you learn that?'

'I heard mum say it, so I asked what it meant. It's got a nice sound – I think it's the "s" coming back at the end, *sarcasssm* - I like it.'

'Yes, it was sarcasm,' said Julia and looked at Anthony, who stood waiting with her glass of wine in his hand. 'Have we got a budding linguist here, do you think?'

'I never heard her say anything like it before,' he said and handed her the glass. 'But a career in languages might save her from a job as an alarm siren. If I go deaf before middle-age we'll know who to blame it on.'

'Now come and sit down with me on the sofa,' said Julia to the children, 'and I'll tell you what happened to me the other day. I went in an ambulance!'

The exclamations and shrieks brought Barb from the kitchen. 'What? And I didn't know? God, Jules, *why* are you so damn secretive? What happened?'

'Nothing major – the ambulance ride was due to a bossy woman who wouldn't let me get up when I was knocked down by a scooter in Rule Street North. If it hadn't been for her I would have just walked away, despite the pain in my head – *so* embarrassing to lie there with people staring at me.' She shuddered dramatically for effect and the children giggled.

She told them the story, interrupted a dozen times by questions from all four members of the Crombie family and at the end, after she had told them about Linda with her leg in traction and her wish to help her, Barb said, just like Prissy had, 'But what could you do for the poor girl?'

Before Julia could reply Barb turned and disappeared saying over her shoulder, 'Sorry! Must check the meatballs!' and from there nothing more was said about it until they sat down to dinner.

'So, what are you planning for that girl?' asked Anthony when they sat down to eat. 'I'm sure there's a spreadsheet in your head with every contingency noted, with full contact details for those who can help. Am I right?'

'You know what? I do object to how you make me sound so boring and stuffy when it's just that I'm usually more organised than … most people. And had you noticed, Barb, how often the word spreadsheet pops up in his conversations these days? Must be these new jobs he has, forced him to get organised. But never mind, you're right, Anthony. And I've got it sorted I think, at least the main points.'

She drank some of her wine and continued, after briefly considering if she should tell them or not, and decided she might as well, or Barb would be even more indignant when she eventually found out. 'If all goes well Linda will be discharged in roughly two weeks provided her traction leg has done whatever it's supposed to do – stretched, I suppose or healed a bit more, or at least not shrunk and got shorter. She can only leave if she goes somewhere safe, with a caregiver visiting to help with showering, because she'll have the leg that was in traction in a cast and the other in a moon boot. I've had the people from the hospital's home-care department inspect my flat and it's been approved – as have I.'

She took a sip of her wine before she continued and thought that this was turning into a long story, but she'd better tell them all the details and surprisingly even the children seemed interested.

'I'm going to get in touch with her parents, who sadly would have nowhere to come back to, even if they could return from Bangladesh to take care of her. Their house in Westport has been let long-term, and all their stuff is in storage. I've spoken to my neighbour, so all that's left now is to talk to Linda. Oh yes, I should add that Linda told me yesterday that she'd rather remain in hospital, boring though it is, than go to her uncle and aunt in Auckland. She says they don't approve of her parents, and they would go on and on about how irresponsible they are, and she couldn't stand it. She hasn't seen them since she was fifteen and spent a two-week holiday with them.'

Barb looked long and hard at her older sister. 'Are you totally bonkers? You went ahead with all this, and you haven't even talked to Linda? Crazy!'

Debbie giggled and whispered, 'She's crazy!' which earned her a push from her brother.

'I've visited her three times since I first met her, and I'm getting to know her reasonably well.

She's mature for her age, very self-possessed though she looks like she's fifteen, and she can relate to people my age and to kids Seb's age, which tells you something. I took some magazines and fruit and sat down for an hour or so each time and got to know her a bit. I'll broach it with her this weekend. And by the way Anthony, did you know you've got a bulge in the sidewall on your offside rear tyre?'

He looked surprised and said, 'But those tyres are quite new! How would that have happened?'

'Could be a couple of things – manufacturing fault, having hit a sharp kerb at a funny angle, heaven knows. But go back to where you got them from before you go on a long trip - they'll sort it out.'

Barb was still full of objections about Julia's plan to take care of Linda and butted in as soon as she could. 'What do you mean, talk to your neighbour? Who's the neighbour? And who is Seb? Really, Julia, you need to explain things a bit more.'

She's like a terrier when she gets her teeth into something, thought Julia, and studied her sister's determined face, she's getting to be nearly as good at interrogation as Helen. I'll just have to carry on.

'She lives in the flat next to mine, she's in her

mid-seventies and we play Scrabble every now and then, or we have a glass of wine with her sitting on her balcony and me on mine. You know how those recessed balconies jut out a little? Just enough for us to have a chat, so we talk across the gap. The neighbours probably listen in or close their windows and think we're mad. She's as fit as a fiddle and likes to have her friends visit her rather than go out, so she's at home most of the time. Sometimes I text her from the supermarket in case I can pick something up for her. Her name's Gwyneth, she's Welsh originally. There! Full disclosure - now you know everything.'

'You *are* the most secretive sister anyone ever had!' exclaimed Barb. 'It's like I don't know a thing about your life. Tragic, really.'

'But what's she got to do with Linda?' Anthony with an amused look, but whether at Julia's revelations about her friendship with the neighbour or at the expression of outrage on his wife's face wasn't clear.

'Oh, I had to reassure the home-care people, the ones who came to inspect the flat, that there'd be some emergency backup on hand if Linda gets into what they call a situation while I'm at work. I talked to Gwyneth, and she said she'd love to be the support person, and she's already got a key to my place. Perfect!'

Anthony shook his head slowly from side to

side the way people do when they find it hard to believe what they just heard. 'My God, Julia, you really are something else! The things you do sometimes blows my mind. You're like a force of nature. And who's Seb?'

'He's the little boy on the scooter who knocked me down, Sebastian. Gorgeous kid - sat beside me on the pavement until the ambulance came and told he his full name in case I wanted to sue him!' She laughed at the memory. 'He and his mum came to the hospital later that afternoon, and he went and sat on Linda's bed, and between them they ate most of the chocolates he'd brought for me. Next time I go I'll take him with me so he can see Linda again.'

'How old is he?'

'He's eight, I think, an only child with a mother who's strict and a dad who's relaxed but often working away for a week at a time.'

When she left, Anthony remained in the open door, so a long streak of light from the hall lit her way along the uneven path to the gate, the way he always did, and Barb joined him calling out a goodbye. Just as Julia reached the gate she heard that non-voice again, like muted words in her mind.

I wonder if she really did break off with that young guy? She didn't mention him this time.

Julia swung around, instinctively ready to respond but was distracted by the wave of pale blue that flowed swiftly through her mind, and when she looked up the door was shut. She remained where she was for a minute and wondered once again if she really had a lasting head injury. This was the third time it had happened, and she knew now that what had come across like a voiced comment was Barb's thought. The feel of it was just like when she was talking to Prissy in the hospital, before she knew what it was, when she thought it was someone in the corridor, but that time it was accompanied by a different colour. And in the restaurant the other day, when she felt she heard Milton Parker's thought and saw a colour. But can you really feel a colour in your mind? Can thoughts have colours? And why was it suddenly happening now when nothing like it had ever happened to her before? It had to be due to the concussion.

She got into her car and drove slowly through the suburban streets towards the centre of town, but after a few minutes she pulled over and parked, unable to concentrate. How did this happen? And why? If the concussion had caused a serious head injury she would have other symptoms, but she had no headaches, her sense of balance was intact and everything was the way it should be, just normal. It must be an isolated and very strange result of the concussion, some kind of psychic ability caused by neurons connecting differently or something. On one level she knew it had to be that because there was no other explanation. On another level she wanted to dismiss it as nonsense, the kind of ideas promoted by people who believed in magic and witches. Hearing a strange, disembodied voice once could be dismissed as a random event, three times had to mean something, and if it was a psychic ability she would have to accept it. But why only a few random thoughts from those particular people?

Eventually she started the car again and drove off, feeling as if she had suddenly taken a wrong turn and ended up in someone else's reality. A place where she didn't know the rules and where logic worked differently.

12

At lunchtime the next day, Morgan came into the office and said, 'He's back, that guy in the red Toyota. He hasn't been here for a few days, but he's sitting outside right now - a bit closer this time, so maybe you shouldn't come into the workshop and look at him. You'd be easier to spot from where he's parked now.'

'OK, I won't go and look at him. Let's just ignore him, don't look for him and don't talk about it. It's not as if he's standing in the doorway being threatening, and nobody's tried to abduct me.'

Morgan frowned. 'You shouldn't joke about it, Julia - we don't know why he's there and until we do, or until he stops, we should take it seriously.'

'I'm sorry.' Julia felt guilty that she had made light of their concern. 'You guys are being so protective - it's very nice of you. I promise I won't go outside and look at that car.'

Rob now joined them with a wrench in his hand. 'Do you want one of us to go and talk to him? Ask him what the hell he's doing and see how he reacts. I wouldn't mind doing it.'

'God, no!' exclaimed Julia, slightly alarmed. 'Please don't do that and certainly not with that wrench in your hand. Let's just wait and see.'

The men went back to the workshop, and Julia I tried to suppress the slight feeling of unease which she felt every time she thought about the man in the red car. Half an hour later Shane stuck his head in the door and said, 'He's left. This time he did a U-turn and drove back the way he came instead of driving past us. I bet he's noticed to us staring at him.'

The following afternoon Julia was standing just inside the first workshop bay, leaning against the wall and watching Shane using the chain hoist to lower the engine back into a Toyota utility truck that had been modified in a way that made the job tricky. She was about to say something complimentary in the silence when he turned off the hoist, but a glimpse of the car turning into the front yard caught her attention, and she straightened up and stared. 'My God, it's a Ford

Edsel!' she exclaimed. 'Who knew there was one of those around?'

She walked through the door to the office and made it to her desk at the same time as a man entered from the yard – it was Milton Parker again.

'Hi,' he said. 'Any chance I could have a quick word with a mechanic? I realise they're busy, but I'm a bit concerned about something, and I just want ask a question.'

'Can you tell me what it's about?'

'I think I need a mechanic,' he said with a slight smile, and she noticed the little quirk at the corner of his eyebrow, and she knew why.

'Did you come in the Edsel? Is it about that slight grinding noise?'

How lucky I heard it in that little moment of total silence when Shane turned off the hoist, she thought. This is going to be fun!

'That's it,' he said, again with that slightly superior tweak of his right eyebrow. 'Very unusual for a woman to know what that car is, or most men for that matter. They haven't been made for decades.'

'Not since about 1958, I think. The noise when you turned left to come into the yard sounds like it could be tight-mesh pinion gears in the diff. I could be wrong, but it didn't sound like a wheel bearing, and it's got to be looked at.'

That shut him up, she thought, but she knew better than to look triumphant or at all pleased with the effect it had on him. After a moment's silence he said, 'Apologies, I was making assumptions for all the wrong reasons. I thought you were the admin person.'

'Oh, I am the admin person,' said Julia coolly. 'And I'm also a trained mechanic with twenty years' experience. Do you work in town? You could leave the car now or we could do it on Friday if today doesn't suit. We've got no gaps between now and then. It will take a few hours, and if it needs a spare part we would need it for longer.'

'Do you think it's safe to drive?'

'Probably, at least until the noise gets worse. But you don't want to strip the pinion gears, so doing it sooner rather than later is a good idea. We should be able to reset the meshing and avoid trouble unless something's already damaged – it's basically an alignment thing. It's taking the diff out and taking it apart that takes the time.'

'I'll bring it on Friday morning and leave it until you tell me it's fixed. I don't need it for transport, it's a toy. Will it be inside and locked up if it's here overnight?'

'Yes, certainly - and we have insurance for cars that are left with us overnight. It's included in our fire and building insurance package.'

He still hasn't smiled properly, she thought, and that eyebrow is driving me wild. He thinks his sarcasm is hidden, doesn't realise it's as clear as daylight. What a pity such a sexy beast is not as handsome on the inside as he is on the outside.

He turned to go, then turned back and said, 'I hope they appreciate how valuable you are in this job.'

'Oh, God yes,' said Julia straight-faced. 'The boss tells me nearly every day.'

'*Gorgeous woman*,' said a muted voice and she jumped. 'Sorry, did you say something?'

He turned again and smiled. 'No, wasn't me,' he said and continued outside. Oh my God, there it was again, thought Julia, he didn't say out loud, and that burgundy colour washed through my mind again, just like that night when I felt his comment about me and Ashton in the restaurant. Same person, same colour. Is this something that happens to other people after concussions? Have I never heard of it because people don't dare tell anyone in case people will think they're mad? That's four times now, or is it five?

As soon as Parker shut the door she heard a snort of laughter and realised Rob was standing in the door to the workshop. 'Well, you had him twisting and turning,' he said. 'That bit about the boss was great. Amazing car!'

'A total disaster of car!' said Julia and tried to

disengage from her internal speculations and sound normal. 'Often referred to as the most expensive mistake in auto manufacturing. I watched a YouTube thing about the Edsel a couple of years ago. They only made them for a couple of years, there were so many problems they just gave up and stopped. Imagine how Henry Ford would have felt if he'd still been alive when they made it. The car was named after his son, who had died before him.'

'Must be worth a mint, though – they can't have made many.'

Julia tried to look relaxed despite the turmoil in her mind. 'A very expensive toy I guess, but I don't know what they're worth. If you find out please tell me.'

Rob went back to his work and Julia's mind immediately reverted to the comment she had heard as Milton Parker was leaving. This time the colour that had briefly appeared in her mind was stronger, a deep vibrant shade, different from the earlier occasions when the colours had been muted. Why did it only happen with some people and not others? There must have been thousands of thoughts in people's heads in her vicinity since her accident, but only those from three people had appeared as spoken words in her head. She kept thinking of the sound of those words. On each occasion it was the same voice, neither male nor female, and there was no distinct intonation;

it was an impersonal, sexless voice. Irritated by at the way she couldn't stop thinking about this, she thought how much she would love to meet someone else who was experiencing the same thing and tried to concentrate on her work.

13

The thought of the man in the red car was a vague worry in the back of Julia's mind for the next couple of days, and though the car had not been seen again, she found it hard to dismiss it. On a morning with a freezing wind after an early frost, which seemed to indicate a long winter ahead of them, Julia drove to her dental appointment instead of walking like she normally would. She hadn't brought her padded jacket and the thought of heading into that blustery wind in a thin coat wasn't inviting, so although finding a place to park might be frustrating, she decided to drive rather than walk. She knew it was unlike her, but lately things had combined to make her feel unsettled, as if the world was conspiring against her. A potential stalker, a sad break-up, a sexy sarcastic man, an ex-partner harassing her. Too much!

On the way back to work she had a sudden idea. It was about the time of day the red car sometimes turned up and as it hadn't been there for a couple of days maybe it would be there today. She drove the long way around and approached the garage from the left, a route she never normally took, and there was the red car, parked in its usual place.

She pulled in half a block behind him and she could see the driver was sitting in the car as usual, so she walked up from behind him, knocked on the passenger door window and pulled the door open, standing well back.

'What are you doing here?' she demanded of the driver who stared at her in surprise. 'You sit here a couple of days each week at roughly the same time, stay for an hour or two and then drive off. Are you stalking someone?'

'No,' he said and then he grinned. 'Well, maybe I am stalking someone, but I never thought of it like that before. I'm conducting surveillance.'

'Of me?'

'God no! Why do you think that?'

'I own the garage over there and the guys who work for me think you might be stalking *me*. I just thought I'd ask.'

Now he laughed and reached behind him,

grabbed his jacket and pulled out a wallet from the inside pocket. 'Here's my licence – I'm a private detective, ex-police, and I'm trying to get some concrete evidence about a guy whose wife thinks he's cheating on her. Why don't you get in out that damn wind – you must be freezing.'

'I hope the guys at work aren't watching this.' Julia got in smiling at the thought. 'If they are, you'll be dragged out of this car in a couple of minutes by three men wielding heavy tools – they'll think you've taken me hostage or something.'

'Hang on a moment while I reverse a couple of spaces so they can't see me.' He backed rapidly nearly all the way to where Julia's car was parked. 'I can still see what I need to see from here. So, your mechanics are very protective of you, are they? Have you had some trouble already?'

'No, not really – at least nothing serious. I didn't realise until they spotted you that they felt concerned. I mean, I'm a grown woman and I've worked with them for years. I had no idea they got concerned about the way some customers kind of … well, they've heard some guys being a bit overly friendly. Which I never thought of – I mean, I didn't think they picked up on stuff like that.'

'Count yourself lucky,' was all he said, his eyes still trained on the street corner ahead of them.

'Tell me about the guy who's cheating on his

wife. This is interesting, I've never met a detective before. Are you going to confront him if he turns up?'

'God, no. I'm just gathering evidence. He parks not far from here, does a little detour on foot to get to the high-rise apartment block up that side street behind your garage, and when I spot him I'll take a photo of him. It's just part of a whole sequence of shots that will prove beyond doubt that he's visiting his mistress in his lunch hour now and then – very long lunch breaks. The wife thinks she knows who it is – a woman who lives up there and works from home, very convenient for them.'

Julia considered this scenario and protested. 'But taking a photo from here doesn't prove anything, does it? He could just say he's going for a walk. Why aren't you outside the apartment building?'

He shot an amused look at her, then his eyes swivelled back to the street. 'You really do like to find out how it works don't you? Maybe you should have been a detective? The reason I'm not sitting outside the apartment block is that it's hard to hang around there without being obvious, nowhere to hide holding a camera, and if he comes on foot from this direction I'll only have a moment to get a shot of him up there. So, what I'm trying to do is get a sequence of images from where he parked his car, which he always does in the same place. I'm convinced he approaches the apartments from this direction sometimes - he varies his routes. And then I want one last shot of him pressing a button on the entry panel at the apartments. But I'd have to blatantly stand in the open and do it and it might be the last time I have a chance to surprise him.'

After thinking this over Julia asked curiously. 'How much money is this wife prepared to spend? You've spent hours just on this location – I bet you're expensive.'

'Money is no problem for her - and this is the only place that links where he parks the car and where he goes, unless he walks right around the block, which he does sometimes. She's prepared to pay for my time to establish that link. Proving he's devious and trying to hide where he goes, not leaving his car outside the block of flats, it all tells a story. When I present the file to her it will have a printed map of this area with the place he parked his car marked, this place marked for the occasions when he uses this approach, and then finally the shot of him pressing the crucial bell on that entry panel at the apartment block. Plus, a photo of the entry panel so it links to where his finger was in the previous photo.'

'Very clever!' said Julia appreciatively. 'You're putting together a whole story with visual evidence that he won't be able to deny.'

'Just like I did when I was a police detective,'

he said and lifted the camera she hadn't paid attention to from the dashboard. 'And would you believe it, there he is now - don't move.' He raised the camera with the long lens and took three rapid shots of the man on the other side of the street. Then he swung the camera to the side and took several shots through the window on Julia's side, as he disappeared up the side street towards the tall block of apartments further up the hill.

'Well, that's the last time you'll see me parked here. You can tell the guys in the garage to relax now.'

'Can I tell them a bit about this - what you've told me?' They'll be so surprised, she thought, and laughed inside at how they'd tell her off and be avid for details at the same time. Priceless, an opportunity not to be wasted.

'So long as you don't mention the client's name or my name which you saw on my licence. I can't afford to have stories circulating about what I'm doing.'

'Of course not. And I don't know the name of those people anyway, and I won't mention where the mistress lives. But my guys will be so interested to hear what you were really doing here. Thanks for filling me in!'

'Nice to talk to you - and tell your mechanics they're doing a great job looking out for you. Don't laugh at them. These things matter.'

Julia got out of his car and walked back to her

own, and by the time she started the engine he had already driven off. When she walked in the back door to the workshop the mechanics were in the lunchroom, so she walked in, made a cup of coffee and sat down at the table.

'Now, I've got a story to tell you, but you've got to be discreet with the information. I've just spent ten or fifteen minutes sitting in the passenger seat of that red car talking to the guy, who's not a stalker, he's a detective on a stakeout.'

Their expressions ranged from outraged to surprised, to amused and made her laugh. At the end of the story and after answering a multitude of questions, she told them about the detective's final comment, how he had said that she was lucky to have such wonderful guys looking out for her.

'And he's right - I might laugh at some of the things you say, but I'm only doing it, so I won't break down and embarrass you by getting emotional.'

14

It was Saturday morning and Julia had just come off the phone after making sure someone would be in the hospital admin office, when a text message arrived. Julia thought only for a moment before she called Prissy. The text from Prissy's phone had been sent by Seb, but whether he had his mother's permission was impossible to tell. Maybe he'd just picked up her phone and decided to contact her the way Debbie sometimes did.

'Hi!' said Prissy when she took the call. 'I hope you're quite recovered now. Did you find out anything useful about Linda?'

'Oh yes, lots of things. I'm going to visit her this afternoon and I wondered if you'd let me take Seb. Linda said how cute he was and what fun it was to talk to someone younger than herself. She's an only child too.'

'Of course, just let me think for a moment. I've got to go to help my dad with his tax return a bit later, he hates doing it online. I've just come back from school where I was doing some voluntary work in the library, we're moving it to a new building and it's tricky – keeping track of the sequence of shelves we're moving.' She paused for a moment and decided to clarify. 'I'm the part-time secretary at Seb's school, I job-share with another woman. I don't think I mentioned it, but the day he knocked you over he was going to get some KFC and then come back to the school and wait for me – I was taking notes at a staff meeting.'

Julia waited, but there was a long pause. 'And?' she said finally, not sure if she was interrupting a thought process or if it was her turn. 'Is it OK if I pick him up in half an hour or so? We'd probably be a couple of hours or a bit more, maybe three.'

'Oh, of course! Sorry, I got side tracked there. I was considering if I could bring him to the hospital on my way to my dad's place and meet you there, so you don't have to go out of your way.'

'Don't worry, it's fine, and much easier than trying to coordinate ourselves in that huge car park – and it's no trouble.'

. . .

'I was going to ask you if you wanted to come anyway,' said Julia when she and Seb were in the car. 'Linda would like to see you, and I've got some stuff to talk over with the admin people at the hospital, so you two can keep each other company while I get that done.'

Sebastian held up a five dollar note. 'I took some out of my savings box so I can buy something nice for her from that shop at the entrance because mum said hospital food isn't very interesting. What do you think she'd like, maybe a cake?'

Julia glanced over at this thoughtful little boy sitting there planning an act of kindness and smiled.

'Funny you should say that. I was going to stop by that supermarket near the hospital and get something from the bakery counter. I thought I'd buy a couple of nice drinks for you and Linda and maybe pastries or something for you two to have while I go and talk to the hospital admin people. They have a great selection there.'

To Julia's surprise Seb asked no questions about why she would visit the office, instead he said, 'Great! They do have nice cakes in that supermarket - can I choose what kind we buy?'

They had made their choices and were nearly at the checkout when Julia remembered something. 'Hang on, Seb – I need to go back to the aisle with canned food.'

Seb stood to one side and watched her piling tins of baked beans and soup into her bag and looked as if he was trying not to laugh when she turned to him and asked him to hold a few. 'What's that for? Is that all you eat – soup and baked beans?'

'No, but I always have a few in the car.' She turned and headed back towards the checkout and Seb followed behind, once again with no further questions. He's so unusual, thought Julia when she offloaded a dozen cans of food on the conveyor belt along with the doughnuts and drinks he had chosen. I don't think I've ever known a child who's so thoughtful and considers things so silently before he comments or asks a question.

'So, are you going to tell me?' Seb glanced her way as he clicked his seatbelt into place. 'All those cans – and you've just thrown them into that carton on the floor in the backseat. Or is it a secret?'

'No, it's not a secret -I offer them to street sleepers. Open the glove box and you'll see all the wooden, disposable spoons I keep there. And did you notice that all the cans have tear-tab tops?'

He was silent for a long time and then finally he said. 'Why? Is it because they're always hungry? Don't they even have enough money to buy food? People do give them money, I've seen it. We give them money sometimes, too.'

'I don't know what they have or don't have, but I never give them money because I think a lot of them would buy alcohol or drugs and still not get enough to eat. So, when I see one I just ask if they'd like some food.'

'But the cans are in the car,' protested Seb. 'Usually, you see those guys sitting outside shops in town or in the park sometimes. How does that work?'

Julia turned into the hospital carpark and smiled. 'Check inside my shoulder bag. It's on the floor on your side.'

A moment later Seb laughed. 'Aha! You just take one every time you get out of the car – and a spoon, don't you?'

'I carry it around until someone accepts it and then I put another one or two in my bag. It's like a mild form of weight training. Sometimes I see one of these guys – and it *is* usually men – asleep on the pavement in the evening, or on a park bench, and then I just leave it beside them, so they'll find it when they wake up.'

'You're very unusual - special,' said Seb seriously.

'So are you, darling. Very special. Remember I said that to you after I fell, and I said you should tell your parents what I'd said in case they got angry with you.'

'Do you say you fell?' He sounded genuinely surprised. 'Don't you say you got knocked over?'

'I did fall,' said Julia and got out of the car. 'Doesn't matter how it happened, does it? Now, if you take the packet of doughnuts I'll take the drink cans, and we'll stop and get me a coffee from the café at the entrance. When I've had my coffee and a quick chat to Linda I'll go and talk the people in the office, and you can entertain her while I'm gone. She likes talking to you.'

After a lengthy chat with the woman in the office who understood exactly what Julia needed to know, a timeline for Linda's discharge had been established. Julia extracted a promise that someone would visit Linda and get her agreement to be released into Julia's care, after which it seemed things should be reasonably straight forward.

'We don't legally need her formal agreement because she's not a minor,' said the woman in the office, 'but I suppose it's a good idea to have her word that she's happy to go home with you, seeing you're not a relation and haven't known her long. She's young after all and her parents are overseas.'

Julia was nearly at the door to Linda's room where she was again the sole patient when she heard Seb's voice and stopped to listen. 'You lost! That's your three guesses used up,' he said gleefully. 'You have to give up because you'll never get it - she gives them to street sleepers!'

Fascinated to hear how Seb would explain the story behind the many cans of food in her car, Julia listened without moving to the exchange that followed. That Seb was good at telling a story soon became clear as he reenacted the entire scene in the car for Linda, from the point where he asked why the cans were on the floor to checking the packets of little wooden spoons in the glove compartment and looking in her bag.

'Hi there,' said Julia and walked in as if she hadn't heard their conversation. 'I think I've got it sorted now. Someone will come and check that you really trust me, and then I'll pick you up after your next meeting with the orthopedic guy in a couple of days.'

'In a wheelchair?' asked Seb who was sitting cross-legged on Linda's bed which was strewn with drawings, doughnut wrappings and drink cans. 'Electric? One of those that can go up and down stairs?'

Linda laughed and poked him in the ribs. 'Wheelchair? So you can ride around in it? Of course not! I'll just need crutches, won't I, Julia? I'll have a moonboot on one leg and some kind of cast on the other leg, so it's not as if I'm a proper cripple, is it?'

'We'll hire a wheelchair and keep it in the car,' said Julia. 'They told me I can get it from the pharmacy in Coulson Street, they hire them out per week. It might be a good thing to have if we make an excursion to do some shopping or something. All the other stuff we'll get from the hospital stores when I pick you up. They'll lend us what they think we'll need.'

Seb was naturally fascinated. 'What other stuff?'

Linda looked at Julia with a silent question, so she said casually, 'A booster toilet seat that goes on top of the regular seat. It makes it higher, so you can get up more easily, and a thing that sits by the bed to steady yourself on when you get up. Just normal things that people need when they have two broken legs. Extra safety gear. And a chair to have in the shower.' She tried to remember what else. 'Oh, yes, and a few of those plastic covers to put over the cast on the stretched leg when you shower. Apparently it's like a big plastic bag with some kind of sticky stuff at the top to seal it.'

'They've already checked my legs are the same length,' said Linda to Seb. 'Imagine if the stretched one had got too long!'

They both broke out laughing and Julia sat back in the visitor's chair and listened to them talking while she thought about her flat and how best to move some of the furniture to make it safer for Linda to move around in.

15

When Julia stopped outside Seb's house he turned to her and said, 'Mum wants to talk to you – did I say?'

'No, I don't think you did. Are you sure she has time for a visitor?'

Seb undid his seatbelt and opened the door and said over his shoulder. 'Of course, she's very interested in Linda, and she said to ask you in. Come on!'

Seb walked straight into the house, saying 'Come on!' again over his shoulder but Julia hesitated on the doorstep. To walk into a house where she had never been before on the say-so of a little boy, however fondly he thought his mother would like to see her, was a step too far.

'Do come in, Julia.' Prissy came out of a door to the left of the hall and reached out as if to take her hand. 'Come in and have a coffee or a glass of wine unless you're busy elsewhere? My husband is out helping a friend fix his garage door, but he'll be home soon.'

The kitchen they entered was at least two generations younger than the house itself, a large space probably made up of the original kitchen and the dining room.

'What would you like?' asked Prissy. 'It's just after five so maybe we could have a wine, if you drink wine?'

'That sounds lovely, thanks.' While Prissy busied herself pouring wine and putting roasted cashew nuts into a bowl, Julie looked around and thought what a great job they had done with this old villa.

'What a lovely room,' she said and took the wine glass Prissy handed her. 'Light coming in from both ends – gorgeous!'

'It did work well, but we had a good designer – he saw things from a bigger perspective than we did, and he thought having this space going right through from one end to the other would make it better than the idea we had. And he was so right because we don't really need a separate space to call a study – this room is our everything-room. Where do you live?'

'In an apartment in that tall block of flats on the corner of Hinton Street people call the glass house.'

'Well, it does look as if it's covered in blue

glass, but I suppose there are solid walls behind the glass. It's an interesting looking building. Are the apartments nice?' Prissy led the way down the room and put the bowl of nuts between them on the padded window seat. 'I remember when they put it up – someone said the lifts are unusual, but I can't remember what it was that makes them special.'

It made Julia laugh. 'You wouldn't believe how many people have asked to come and see the lifts since I moved in. I made a video of my trip to the third floor to show my sister in Hawke's Bay – posted it on Facebook. I'll show you.'

Prissy took the phone Julia passed to her, watched the video and called to Seb. 'Where are you Seb? Come and look at what Julia just showed me.'

'Trees?' said Sebastian disbelievingly a few minutes later after playing the video twice. 'Are there trees inside your building somehow? It looks awesome.'

Julia watched him start the video clip again and smiled. 'It's a great lift, best one I've ever been in. That display is just a blank opaque glass wall like a huge TV screen with the shadows of those tree canopies somehow played on it, it's not real trees, but it looks as if you're rising up through super tall trees.'

'Will you show me one day?' asked Sebastian and then added quickly, 'I don't mean you have to invite me to your place, but maybe we could just go up and down in the lift?'

Julia smiled at this polite way of inviting himself without being intrusive. 'As soon as Linda moves in you'll be able to come and visit and spend time with her. She'll need company, and she can help you with your homework too. She said you told her you don't like mathematics and it's a subject she's good at herself, so she might be quite useful. And if you want to you can go up and down in the lift as many times as you like. When my niece and nephew come to visit they usually go up and down three or four times before they actually come to see me.'

Prissy was shaking her head from side to side very slowly the way people do when they find something hard to believe. 'You're like a fulltime entertainment programme, Julia. Are you married?'

'No, I'm not. I was in a relationship a while back, but it ended after less than two years. Maybe I'm not marriage material.'

'You'd be a great mum.' Seb looked seriously at her. 'You should be married, you're such fun to be with.'

'Thank you,' said Julia and took her phone back. 'You are great fun to be with, too.'

Prissy had just started saying something when the sound of the front door closing made her look up and a tall, gangly man carrying two shopping bags came into the kitchen.

'I wondered who that car belonged to. You must be the poor woman Seb knocked over. I'm Gordon. I'm very pleased to meet you, I've heard a lot about you lately.'

Julie got up to shake his hand and said casually, 'Oh, we don't refer to it as being knocked over. Seb and I have agreed that it was equally much my fault as his and we now refer to it as when I fell over - I have to accept my share of the blame after all.'

The only way she could think of to prevent Seb from feeling forever guilty about the accident, which she knew he still did, was to change how it was referred to; she hoped it would work.

An hour later Julia drove home thinking that she must introduce Seb to Debbie and James. He was much the same age as James but a very different kind of boy, more thoughtful and more attuned to adults, which was probably a consequence of being an only child. She felt very close to Seb, very much the way she felt about James and Debbie, as if she was connected by blood to him as well. She knew that if she could have chosen anyone in the world to knock her over and give her this strange concussion that had changed her life she couldn't have picked anybody better then Sebastian. Getting to know him had added a new dimension to her life, which somehow compensated for the scary strangeness of the thoughts she heard. And don't forget the colours, she reminded herself, they're as strange and scary as hearing people's thoughts.

16

When Helen called late one afternoon and said how about they meet for a drink straight after work because she had something to tell her, Julia said she would be there at half past five, and only later thought that she should have suggested a different place to meet. But it was a busy day, and she didn't take the time to text Helen and suggest a change, so just after five she set out for Ben's Bistro again wondering what it could be that Helen wanted to tell her; straight after work on a weekday was an unusual day to meet. Slightly uneasy she hoped it wasn't going to turn out to be bad news about health or some marriage problem which Helen hadn't wanted to talk about on the phone.

As usual Julia parked the car in the supermarket car park, pulled up the collar of her jacket and made a mental note to put her merino scarf in the car because the collar turned up wasn't the same as warm layer of wool around her neck. When she was only a short distance from the supermarket a car slowed down beside her and a voice called out, 'I'll give you a lift.'

It was the Edsel with Milton Parker at the wheel. 'Hop in!' he said. 'It's a cold night to be out walking.'

'I don't mind the cold,' said Julia, surprised that he had stopped to offer her a lift. Of all the people who might have spotted her walking, he would have been the last she would have expected to offer her a ride. But he didn't drive away, just continued driving slowly beside her.

'Please get in,' he said seriously, with emphasising on please. 'This isn't a safe neighbourhood these days, and I really don't like the look of that guy in the hoodie who followed you from the supermarket carpark.'

Julia swung around but couldn't see anybody behind her. 'There's nobody there,' she said slightly irritated at Milton's persistence.

'I can see him in the mirror,' said Milton looking into the rearview mirror as he spoke. 'He stopped walking when you did, and now he's standing just inside the shelter at the bus stop, probably waiting for me to drive away. Please get in and I'll take you to wherever you're going.'

Julia couldn't turn down the opportunity to

go for a ride in the Edsel, a chance that might never come her way again. She had driven it into the workshop once, but the chance to go for a drive on the street was irresistible. The front bench seat was long enough to seat three adults and the dashboard glowed with the same bright turquoise enamel as the outside of the car, with shiny chrome edges on the large round dials. It was even more compellingly different at night with the dash brightly lit. Completely different from a modern car, like stepping back into a bright and shiny past. Perhaps into a safer and less difficult time than the present, she thought, like being in a capsule of solid glamour.

'It's a glorious car,' she said. 'And thanks for offering me a ride. I'm going to Ben's Bistro a couple of blocks down from here to meet a friend.' Then she realised that parking at the supermarket and walking would seem very strange, so she added, 'She always suggests this place and I've been going to ask her to meet me somewhere else because parking by the bistro is probably worse than parking in the supermarket car park and walking.'

'Definitely,' said Milton decisively. 'I spotted you walking across the car park when I came out of the supermarket, and I saw that guy watching you and then setting out after you - it just didn't feel right.'

'I'm very grateful,' said Julia. 'Oh, here we are. Thank you so much for the ride.'

'Get your friend to drop you back to your car,' said Milton when she got out. She stood on the pavement and watched him drive away and realised she had been so intent on studying the Edsel's interior that she hadn't once looked closely at his face, and if she wasn't watching his eyebrow she couldn't tell if he was being sarcastic. Sarcastic but kind, she corrected herself, very thoughtful.

Inside she found Helen at the same table as last time, and Julia was relieved to see she looked perfectly normal, not at all stressed or worried.

'What's up?' she asked. 'Is it rugby night again or why are we meeting in the middle of a week?'

Helen laughed. 'I didn't know where to go, I'm homeless. I've decided that the boys have to learn to cook, so they've been told they have to make dinner one night a week instead of spending all their free time in front of a device. They came home from school today, and they'd obviously had a talk about it on the way home, and I was given an ultimatum. I have to stay out of the kitchen, and preferably out of the house, while they work. They said they know I'll just hang around and watch every move they make, and it will drive them crazy. They told me they demand the right to be creative on their own.'

'Great idea! Are they working as a team or are

they making separate things, like one making a meat dish and the other veg and potatoes?'

'They're working as a team. I thought it would be good for them to learn how to do something together that neither of them knows very much about - you know, cooperate and fit in with each other and work it out. Tonight, they have the choice of lamb chops with mashed potatoes or fried fish and potato wedges – or the other way around. Their choice of veg, there's lots in the freezer. And if they don't want to make either of those dinners they can raid the freezer and the pantry and do something else. So, instead of sitting in the living room reading or watching TV I got right out of the house.'

'I suppose the temptation to sneak up to the kitchen door and check what they were doing would be hard to resist. I know how bossy you are, and you'd never believe they could work out how to do it right if you didn't tell them.'

'Exactly,' said Helen. 'So here we are. What have you been up to lately?'

'Oh, lots of things. I can't remember when we last caught up and what I told you then, but I've got an injured teenager who's recovering from a bad accident moving in with me in a couple of days, she broke both legs, so that's been a bit of a mission getting things set up. And I fell over in the street and got concussed, but no serious damage. That's how I got to know Linda, the girl with broken legs. And the guys at work thought I had a stalker. Oh yes, one of our customers picked me up on the way here because he thought a guy in a hoodie was following me from the supermarket car park.'

'Christ!' exclaimed Helen. 'That's going to take a bit of time to tell, I mean all the details. What did you do to end up concussed?'

'Oh, I just fell over in the street, turned suddenly right in front of a kid on a scooter and that was it – bang! But I'm all better now so don't worry about it. And the injured kid who's coming to stay is a Polytech student whose parents are working overseas. She's got nowhere to go to recuperate and learn to walk properly again.'

Helen looked seriously at her across the table and said in a slightly disbelieving voice, 'This sounds completely mad, Julia. All these things happening in the few weeks since we last met, and you haven't told me any of it. Aren't we best friends? Shouldn't I know if you've been in an accident?'

Was she serious? She sounded slightly hurt, and Julia realised that maybe most people would have shared all this with their best friend instead of waiting until the next time they met.

'I'm sorry,' she said and decided the best thing right now was a little social lie to make Helen feel better. 'I hadn't told anyone and Barb was very cross with me when I told her on visit the other day. But I've been so flat out at work and getting things organised for Linda to come and stay. It's not as if a girl with two broken legs can function unless you organise things properly. If you hadn't contacted me I would have called you to make a date for this weekend or just told you on the phone. I had it all stored up, but I knew it would take at least an hour to tell you about all these things and far more than that if I included all the details. Not to mention all the questions I knew you'd ask, so let's say two hours.'

'What about the stalker? Is he the one who followed you tonight?'

'Oh God, no. The guy tonight was some random creep who tagged along from the supermarket. And the stalker wasn't a stalker at all, he was a private detective on a stake-out. And please don't look like that - he wasn't spying on me, he was doing surveillance for a matrimonial case, but the guys at work got anxious when they saw the same car park just down the road several times. Particularly as the driver just sat there doing nothing for a couple of hours and then drove off.'

'And?' Helen looked suspicious. 'How did you find out he was a detective and not a stalker? I don't suppose he had a logo on his car door, did he?'

Here we go, thought Julia, now she's going to

tell me off again. Have we ever met without her telling me off at least once?

'Oh, that was easy,' she said casually, trying to make it sound reasonable. 'I just walked up to his car and talked to him, asked him what he was doing and told him the guys in the garage thought he was stalking me. We had a very interesting conversation. We sat in his car for ages, and he told me lots of things about his job, which I'd never known before - well I've never known a detective, but I do now.'

'You're totally crazy,' said Helen and shook her head again. 'You really are. I think they missed installing the self-protection module when they assembled you. So, tell me what you learned from the detective.'

'How long have you got until that dinner is ready?'

'The agreement is that we'll eat at half past seven, so you can tell me all about the detective now.'

When they parted an hour later Helen dropped Julia back to the supermarket and she drove home, deep in thought about her short car ride with Milton. It wasn't only the interior of the Edsel that had made her feel so safe, as if she was in a little capsule, isolated from the world, it was Milton himself. And the strange way she felt pulled towards him, how she had nearly reached out across that long bench seat and touched his arm, as if this was something she had done many times before on car rides in the dark, a way to casually and physically connect. He was a man she didn't really know, a man who seemed to find her slightly something-or-other which brought out that sarcastic tweak of his eyebrow, and on her side she had this feeling of strong connection. She had registered this disturbing feeling at the time and pushed it to one side; too confusing to dwell on while in his company. But now her contradictory feelings towards him revolved in her head on endless repeat. Was it really possible to know that someone regarded you as a bit ridiculous and still be deeply attracted to them? And not only physically attracted, because that didn't include liking them, but emotionally attracted. Nothing will come from this, she told herself. It simply can't because even if those thoughts of his that I heard mean he's attracted too, it's only physical attraction and my deeper feelings would make me vulnerable, put me at a disadvantage.

17

Realising that getting organised for Linda's arrival would need at least a full day away from work, Julia contacted Chris, her regular reliever. She was a friend of Gwyneth's who before she retired had been a doctor's receptionist. Chris was impervious to the teasing of the mechanics, understood the computer booking system and was willing to step in whenever Julia needed time off. She happily manned the desk when Julia took leave, so as soon as she had organised when and where to pick up the supplies she needed for Linda, she called Chris, who said she would be happy to come in the next day and the day after if needed.

Thank God I've got a large SUV, thought Julia the next day when she loaded supplies and returned to her apartment. Her spare room had already been reorganised with the bed slightly off-centre against the end wall to give Linda more space to move around without knocking into things. The strange little contraption the hospital had lent her for Linda to support herself when she got out of bed took no room at all. The base of it simply slid under the bed leaving the part to lean on right up against the side of the mattress. The shower chair would live in the walk-in shower which was big enough for them to move around it. And she would make it a rule that Linda could only have showers when Julia or Gwyneth was in the flat if the homecare people couldn't come. Julia had a feeling that the homecare arrangement was prone to glitches, mainly from things she had read in the newspaper, so being extra safe seemed a good idea. The thought of Linda lying injured and helpless on the bathroom floor for hours was intolerable. I've never been this obsessed with safety in my whole life, she thought, standing in the bathroom door as the little mental video clip of Linda falling played out in her mind. But she's someone else's child and I'm responsible for her.

The raised toilet seat and the suction hand grips where easier to deal with. The seat could stay on the toilet all the time and when Julia used the toilet she would simply lift it off and then put it back, and the suction handles seemed to adhere well to the tiled wall. She tested them by pulling hard from different angles and decided they were safe enough. The final item was the wheelchair she had rented from the pharmacy, and it could stay in the back of the SUV for possible shopping expeditions or for an excursion somewhere.

Walking around the apartment looking at everything with Linda's safety in mind made Julia realise how many trip hazards and obstacles there were, things she negotiated without thought. Someone with two broken legs, starting to move around on crutches and learning to regain their sense of balance would be vulnerable to things she herself took for granted. Two legs in so-called moon boots would have been bad enough, but the leg that had been in traction was now going to be encased in a different kind of cast and had to be protected from accidental damage.

Finally, she sat down with a cup of coffee and a sandwich for her late lunch, going over her mental list of tasks and absently studying the kitchen bench. After a moment she got up and moved the electric jug to a different and safer position before she called the student accommodation where Linda had been staying before her accident to ask if she could come and pick up her belongings that afternoon.

'Of course,' said the hostel supervisor, who had introduced herself as Bridget. 'We've got her things safely locked away in a storeroom. And how is she getting along? It sounded like a very bad accident from what I read in the paper.'

'Yes, very bad, but now I think she's getting on fine,' said Julia. 'She's moving in with me tomorrow or the next day, but she'll be on crutches for some time until the leg that was in traction has regained its strength. Then lots of physiotherapy to get her back to normal, but I'm sure she'll be able to pick up her studies again in a couple of months.'

'That probably means starting over next year. She'll have been away too long and a lot of the work she missed has involved practical experience in the field - and there's no way for her to catch up with that by reading,' said Bridget. 'But her course supervisor will make sure they keep a place for her in the next intake, or she can join the course part way through the year at the point she dropped out. I think they're quite flexible.'

'We'll have to wait and see. It's not a thing I can decide, and Linda might not know yet what she wants to do, but it's good to know she can return one way or the other. I'll come by in an hour and pick up her things if you can have somebody available to show me where to find them.'

Julia spent the rest of the afternoon unpacking Linda's belongings, putting clothes in the wardrobe and the chest of drawers, books on the shelves she had emptied the night before, and toiletries easily accessible in the bathroom. It felt funny unpacking somebody else's personal belongings in their absence, but rather than risk Linda trying to do it she decided that she would simply ask her to forgive her for delving into her things to avoid an accident. At half past five, she flattened six cartons and put them in the hall, ready to take down to the recycling dumpster and texted Gwyneth to ask if she wanted to come for a glass of wine and to see what she had organised for Linda.

'You're going to be her backup person and I'd like you to know where everything is and what I've done. And in addition, I think we need to have a plan for the day Linda arrives.'

'Here,' said Julia when Gwyneth arrived and handed her a glass of red wine. 'Let's have a look at what I've done in Linda's room. I think it's good if you know where everything is, in case you need to help her find something, and you might have some ideas about how to organise it a bit better once she's arrived. It's all going to be new to Linda too, and maybe I haven't put things where she'd expect them to be.'

Gwyneth made no comment on how Julia had arranged Linda's belongings apart from saying it was exactly as she would have done it herself.

'Come and sit down in the living room now

and I'll get some cheese out.' Julia knew that Gwyneth didn't like drinking wine on an empty stomach, so they usually had cheese and crackers or nuts. 'I haven't got any nuts, I forgot to buy more when I shopped the other day.'

'I'd feel happier if you got to know each other right from the start,' said Julia a few minutes later and helped herself to a piece of Brie. 'I want Linda to feel comfortable enough to call or text you and ask for help when she needs it. The last thing I want is for her to struggle, to think she can only ask you for help if it's something serious.'

'Heavens, no, we can't have that.' Gwyneth raised her glass of red wine in a toast. 'I'll make sure she knows I'm nearly always at home and I'm only a few steps away. I'll take care to keep in touch with her by text even if she doesn't ask for help, so she gets used to regarding me as practically in the same apartment.'

'You're a star,' said Julia. 'Thank you! I would never have dared take this on if you hadn't been next door and so ready to help.'

'I think it's going to be fun.' Gwyneth's smile was genuine. 'It's years since I had anything to do with a teenager, and I'm sure she's got lots of things to teach me, probably things I've never heard of before. I'm really looking forward to it.

My own nieces and nephews are all approaching middle age now and none of them live here.'

18

After several frustrating phone calls to the City Council, which left her none the wiser about how long it would be until they could process her consent application for adding another two bays to the workshop, Julia decided that walking in with no appointment and simply asking to talk to someone might yield better results.

An hour later and satisfied with what information she had managed to winkle out from reluctant officials, she crossed the fourth floor foyer towards the lift deep in thought about her project. From halfway across the space, she noticed that the lift was stationary at level two and by the time she was pressing the button to go down it still hadn't moved. Impatient to get back to work Julia considered finding the emergency stairs instead of waiting and then changed her mind on the thought that the moment she found the stairs the lift was bound to arrive. A man came up beside her and said casually, 'Going down?'

'Yeah, but the lift seems to be stuck on level two.'

'Do you work here? Heading out for a coffee?' It was a tone of voice she knew well; a casual attempt to pick a woman up hoping for who knows what.

'No, I've got to get back to work,' she said firmly without turning her head. A faint whiff of unwashed clothes came off him, she glanced sideways and recognised him immediately - this was the weirdo who filmed women in toilets. She thanked her lucky star that he had never seen her at the garage, so there was no risk of a confrontation on the off-chance that he had found out who had reported him. What were the odds of meeting him in real life? The look on his face was one she knew well after training and working in a male dominated environment for a couple of decades. This was a guy who fancied himself and thought his coming on to women would flatter them. She suppressed a shudder of distaste at the thought of having any contact with him, but before she could make up her mind to walk away the lift arrived.

As she stepped inside she once again heard that disembodied voice in her head and the deep red colour flowed briefly across her senses. *Gorgeous backside too*. Milton Parker was approaching from the side, three steps from the lift, which made her feel as if fate was interfering in her life, setting her up for yet another coincidence, however unlikely that seemed. Quickly she put a hand over the edge of the door stop it closing in Milton's face and he made it in, and the door slid shut the moment she let go. Within a second of starting the descent the lift stopped with a sudden jerk and the light went out.

'For fuck's sake,' said the unwashed guy. 'Aren't these things supposed to have emergency lighting? What do we do now? Got your phone with you, doll?'

Julia said calmly, 'We wait, I suppose – it will probably start up again in a minute.'

'Why don't I come over to your side? We could have kiss and a cuddle to pass the time – you look like a nice handful.'

She heard him moving, then an arm came across her body and pushed her hard into the corner and Milton said firmly, 'Keep your distance, mate. If you get any closer I'll have to do something you won't like.'

He took a step back until he was so close in front of Julia that she could feel the heat from his body blocking her into the corner. His hand reached back and touched her hip as if to make sure she was fully out of reach.

'Where the fuck did you come from? Want a fight, do you?' The man's voice was taunting, as if he felt sure he'd win any confrontation with Milton, though he obviously hadn't seen him, or he wouldn't have made his kiss and cuddle offer. Milton's hand was still on Julia's hip, and though it made her feel safe, she felt seriously concerned about the prospect of a fight. That brute looked as if he'd be a dirty fighter, and he had the height and the weight to do real damage. Julia put her hand against Milton's back, slid it up to his shoulder to balance herself and got up on tiptoes with her mouth just beside his ear. And even in this strange situation, her mind registered the feel of him under her hand, how his muscles flexed under her palm, a sensation she would revisit later.

'Don't,' she whispered nearly soundlessly, still with her hand on his shoulder. 'Let it go – please.'

'I don't think a fight is necessary,' said Milton, and Julia sensed more than felt his muscles again reacting to her hand. 'But anyone who comes on to my woman like you just did is taking a risk. So just back off a bit and we'll check if there's an emergency phone we can use.'

Just then the light came back on, and the threatening guy looked at Milton, did a stunned-looking doubletake and faced the door without a word. The lift made a little jump and they continued their downward journey in total silence. Milton remained where he was, blocking Julia into the corner, and she let her hand drop and waited. When the door slid open on the ground floor the smelly man left immediately and disappeared at a fast pace towards the exit, Milton moved away from Julia, and they both got out.

'Sorry,' he said. 'I hope I didn't hurt you when I pushed you, but I had to do something to stop that shit.'

'No, you didn't hurt me, and thank you for intervening. That was very quick thinking. I'm glad I wasn't alone with him.'

'You held the door open for me - it was teamwork,' said Milton. 'I don't think he'd seen me get in. He was facing the control panel and a second later the lights went out.'

'I know him ...' they spoke at exactly the same moment, then both stopped and waited for the other to speak.

'You start,' said Milton. 'You know this guy?'

'I don't actually know him, I haven't met him before, but I reported him to the police not long ago for something quite nasty, very nasty, but he doesn't know my face. If I'd thought he'd recognise me, I wouldn't have got into the lift with him for anything. He's a pervert and I don't think he's safe. So, you know him too?'

'He worked for us for a few months a couple of years ago. we sacked him for violence in the workplace and making threats to the one of the admin staff. Everyone was pleased to see him leave. He's not a guy who makes friends wherever he goes.'

They were still standing just beside the lift, and Julia suddenly realised they were very close together, much closer than most people would be comfortable with. It felt as if they were in a bubble of privacy in the middle of that busy, noisy space. And the feeling she had experienced in the dark lift came back to her; how she had steadied herself with a hand on his shoulder to whisper her plea not to start a fight and felt his muscles flex under her palm. How tempted she had been to touch his neck, to feel his skin under her hand. Her feelings about

Milton were confusing and made up of many contradictory parts. Complex impressions interwoven and overlapping and hard to make sense of. There were his thoughts that disconcertingly filtered into her mind, the tone of those thoughts and the sarcastic quirk of his eyebrow when he smiled, but also how kind he had been to pick her up when he noticed the man following her from the carpark the other night. Not to mention the way she had felt pulled towards him in the car, how she had nearly reached out and touched him though he had displayed no particular interest in her. And now, added to those conflicting impressions and feelings, he had protected her once again, and he had been effective in a fast and decisive way that had impressed her.

Her hand moved slightly towards him, as of its own volition, as if she was about to touch him again, and she sensed his instinct to move a fraction closer, then his fingers briefly touched hers. She stared into his eyes for long moments and wondered what was happening to her, this strange sensation of being physically pulled towards him as if by a gravitational force. The silence lasted for what seemed like an eternity while they just looked at each other.

Then Milton took a step back and said, 'I'm glad I was there, but I must go.' He turned on his heel and walked away towards the entrance, and Julia remained where she was for a moment, confused and conflicted, and watched him disappear across the forecourt with the chilly wind ruffling his thick hair.

The way he had touched her hand, however briefly, was deeply confusing. How had he known her hand had moved towards him without looking down, when she herself had hardly realised she had reached out by just a fraction, and he had been looking straight into her eyes? And was that his actual thought she had heard earlier, like what he would have said if he had spoken aloud, or was it not his words, just a feeling of his that translated itself into words in her mind? And what about the colours, how did that work and what did the colours mean?

Julia thought of the night she had walked down Barb's path and heard her thought in her mind. It was the same thing then, and so was Milton's comment when he left her office the day he brought the Edsel in. Each time a flow of colour had washed briefly across her senses, like seeing colour inside her closed eyelids, though her eyes were open. Was it something to do with doors? But no, she realised as she walked out the glass doors into a swirl of cold air, it had nothing to do with doors. In the restaurant with Ashton, she had felt Milton's thoughts about them, and neither they nor Milton were near the door at the time.

'Stop it! You're going to drive yourself crazy!' she said aloud as she unlocked her car, and a man walking past saluted her and laughed and continued on his way without comment.

19

*I*t was one of those days when everything seemed to conspire to create problems that in a rational world wouldn't exist. A couple of customers had spent much longer than necessary explaining in excruciating detail what they thought their car problems were. As usual Julia had listened patiently for as long as seemed reasonable before suggesting they leave it to the mechanics to work out. One man simply walked into the workshop and made Shane come outside with him, to listen to the explanation and discuss what needed to be done. The carefully worded intervention by Julia enabled Shane to go back to what he was doing and to some degree soothed the impatient customer.

But the woman, who spent a long time trying to describe the strange noise her car had made while Julia listened and felt the chance of a late lunch slipping further and further away, tested her impatience to the limit. When the customer finally decided that the noise she had heard had most closely resembled her smoothie blender running at high speed, Julia said, 'Really? That's interesting. Is this a constant noise or just now and then?'

'Oh no, not constant,' said the woman as if Julia was a bit stupid. 'Of course not! It only happened once. I think it was yesterday. No, it might have been the day before, and it was only for a minute or two. I just thought it was best to have it looked at.'

Julia tried to control her mounting impatience and suppressed thoughts of how much she needed to get done that day. Not least the urgent need to forward the additional material the City Council had asked for in relation to her building consent application.

'Leave it with us,' she said. 'Are you going for a walk, or would you like to be dropped home?' Please don't say you want to be dropped home, she prayed silently, we simply don't have the time.

But to Julia's relief the customer opted to go for a walk and said she would be back in an hour or perhaps a bit longer. She then started a meandering monologue about whether she should maybe go and have coffee somewhere, settled for being away two hours and promptly changed it to three, so Julia gently took the car key out of her hand and went out to drive the car into an empty service bay.

'Do whatever you like,' she said quietly to Morgan. 'This is a non-existent problem that needs some kind of rational sounding solution that I can present to the customer when she returns - provided she ever leaves the office. I think what she heard for a *one* minute, once, two days ago was some external noise. There is clearly no problem, so you can make up whatever you like.' She gave him a wry smile. 'She'll be happy as long as she has something she can call it when she talks about it to her husband - which she will do endlessly and repeatedly tonight and probably most of tomorrow.'

Morgan laughed. 'One of those, huh? We seem to have had a run of them lately. Remember that guy a couple of weeks back, who said he thought his front outside wheel was going to fall off and then he came back the next day and asked us to check it again?"

Back in her office Julia found two new customers waiting and resumed being the smiling front face of the business while impatience seethed inside her. Some days her customer face was so close to slipping she nearly had to hold it in place with both hands.

.   .   .

Julia got out of the lift with her dripping umbrella clutched under one arm, two supermarket bags in one hand and her shoulder bag slipping off her wet shoulder. Her attempt to find her keys in bottom of the bag was unsuccessful, so she gave up, let everything slip to the floor and cursed silently under her breath. When her phone issued a muted signal she ignored it as being low priority. Fifteen minutes later, with the shopping in the fridge, the dripping umbrella leaning into the corner on the balcony, and her wet jacket hanging in the shower, she remembered the bag she had dropped in the hall and pulled the phone out.

After a day like the one she had just had she nearly always got changed the minute she walked in the door at the end of the day, got into scruffy comfortable clothes and sat down with a glass of wine before she thought about what to have for dinner. But even that simple plan seemed doomed to failure because on her phone was a very long voice message from Barb:

I tried to call you twice but only got to voice mail. Both kids have come down with Covid, not very sick but running a fever and out of action as far as school goes and any social life in this house is also on hold. I bet we'll all get it now. I haven't checked the recommended timeframe, but I think we'll keep out of everyone's way for a week or two and make sure we don't spread this. They've both lost their sense of smell which has made for some very descriptive observations about the benefits of not being able to smell anything in the bathroom after their father has been there. Carol is in town, but only for two days, and we were going to meet tonight for a drink and possibly dinner, just the two of us, to catch up and compare notes on love, life and the universe. But that's not going to happen, so could you please take my place. If you say yes I'll owe you big time. I don't want her to spend one of her precious evenings in New Zealand alone.

'This is definitely the longest voice message I've ever received, and I haven't the slightest idea who this Carol person is,' said Julia when she called Barb to get some clarification, and what she heard made her laugh.

'Carol used to be Carl,' said Barb and giggled. 'I might not have told you - I only found out a year or so ago. He was in my class at school, I mean *she* was in my class at school, and we were very good friends. I'm sure you remember him, he came out to our place on his bike sometimes. He has since transitioned and become a woman and lives in California.'

'Oh yes, I do remember him. He was that gorgeous looking guy with bright blue eyes, wasn't he? I remember him turning up at home now and then. How long has he, sorry, she been a woman?'

'I haven't the slightest idea, but someone I'm friends with on Facebook got us re-connected. I hadn't had anything to do with him, sorry, I mean her for years. She's only in New Zealand for two weeks catching up with friends. Her family lives somewhere else now and she's on her last few days down here before she flies out. Anyway, it seems a shame to let her down, so can you do it?'

Julia thought for a moment and decided that this surprising little social event might be just what she needed after her frustrating day. 'OK, give me give me her phone number and tell me where you were supposed to meet her, or perhaps just send her a text and say I'm meeting her instead of you. I'll change into dry clothes and do what I can to keep this newly minted woman happy.'

Less than an hour later Julia sat at a little round table in the cocktail bar of a hotel, which took pride in being exclusive and outrageously expensive, where she had never set foot before. The decor of the bar was stunning, silver and black with red accents, very Hollywood and beautifully lit by wall scones. Like a scene in an Art Deco era film, she thought and took a sip of her wine, thoroughly enjoying this different and glamourous place after her exhausting day. Five minutes later, a stunning blond woman dressed in a very tight lime green dress strode into the bar on four-inch heels and paused beside the bar, her gaze swept around the room, then she headed straight for Julia's table.

'Julia!' she exclaimed in a seductive mezzo voice. 'My God, you look nearly the same as you did last time I saw you, must be close to twenty years ago.'

It was hard to believe that this feminine and slightly too thin apparition had ever been a male called Carl, however pretty she had been as a boy.

'It's lovely to see you after all this time!' Julia got to her feet and received two air kisses, one on each cheek. 'And you don't look at all the same as last time I saw you. You look amazing, just gorgeous. If it wasn't for those bright blue eyes of yours I would never believe you're the same person.'

'I was so sorry to hear about Barb's family being struck by Covid. I suppose the kids will miss not being able to go to school and see their friends, but Barb said they're not particularly sick, she's just keeping them all out of circulation.

'I'm sure they'll be fine, but the children might drive her mad of course. She'll be working from home because Anthony is away again and trying to work with those two around and no one else to distract them won't be easy.'

'Are they very naughty?' asked Carol. 'Like, do they fight?'

'No, they're just normal kids, six and nine years old, a boy and a girl. The boy baits the girl and she's got a screech like an alarm siren, so nothing out of the ordinary, I don't think.'

Carol laughed. 'I wouldn't know what kids behave like these days – I never see any. I'll go and get myself a drink, back in a moment.' Julia remained at the table and watched the barman, clearly entranced, talking and smiling as he poured Carol a drink. On the way back to the table several pairs of male eyes followed her every step.

'You do realise, don't you,' said Julia and tried not to laugh, 'that every single man in this place has his eyes firmly fixed on you and not on whoever they're with. Are you married or do you have a partner?'

'I haven't had time.' Carol grinned. 'I've been so busy with my career and with all the various things you have to do, or have done to you, to do the full transition. It's very time consuming. I only decided to do it five years ago and I knew it involved a lot of procedures, but the reality was exhausting and often tedious. I occasionally go out with someone but nothing permanent and at the moment nothing at all.'

'Barb didn't tell me anything about you. What is it you do? '

'I'm a romance writer. Don't laugh – it seems to strike a lot of people as funny. I've been doing it for years. I write under three different names and I'm very successful and earn a lot of money.'

'Why three different names? Is it because you write different types of books under those names?'

'Well yes, it kind of evolved over the years. I started out writing male gay romance, then I started writing female gay romance and now I write trans romance. I kind of felt when I change genres the first time that I needed to be a different person. You know what I mean, a man with a man's name writes about males, a woman with a woman's name writes about women and now I write the trans stuff under my own name.'

She looked at Julia in a considering sort of way, as if she was reassessing her or perhaps trying to fit the image of to the memories she had from high school.

'You were always pretty, I remember your curly black hair and long legs, but now – wow! you're totally beautiful,' she said after a minute of silent scrutiny. 'You were several years older than me and Barb, and I never got to know you, I just knew you as Barb's older sister. Let me guess - I bet you work in the fashion industry or perhaps for a cosmetics company? She paused briefly with her head tilted to one side. 'Or maybe TV?'

Julia somehow managed to keep a straight face, though inside she was laughing because this was one of the funniest conversations she'd had in a long time. 'No, nothing so glamourous,' she said and felt a grin breaking out. 'I'm a mechanic.'

'What!?' Carol's shout of laughter and loud exclamation had every head in the bar turned in her direction.

'No, it's true, I promise.' Julia joined in her laughter. 'I left school at seventeen and became an apprentice at a garage and stayed there for a few years and saved like crazy. And then I went out on my own when I was twenty-three, hired a small space that had been an auto electrician 's workshop and started building a business. It took off amazingly quickly, so now I own my own premises with a four-bay workshop with hoists and pits and every piece of machinery you can think of. I employ three mechanics and hardly ever crawl under a car myself.'

'How utterly amazing!' Carol reached across the table and put a hand on top of Julia's. 'You're an absolute star, the most surprising person I've met in a long time. So, do you work in the office at the garage, or do you just have someone else run it?'

'Oh no, I'm the receptionist and office lady, and I doubt that very many of my customers realise that I own the place.'

'What do they say when they find out? asked Carol clearly hoping for some funny stories, and impulsively Julia decided to tell her about Milton Parker driving his Edsel into the forecourt and saying he thought he'd better talk to a mechanic. When she related what her reply had been she thought Carol might fall off her chair she was laughing so hard.

'God, that's hilarious! Can I put it in a book? You've just given me the most wonderful idea. I've been wondering what my next book should be about. I make a point of giving all my main characters different backgrounds and occupations, and I research all my facts and try and get everything just right. The last one was about a professional Formula One photographer – great job for a trans woman because all the other photographers were men.' She thought for a moment. 'I think I'd like to write a book about a woman mechanic, who runs a big garage. *Please* let me use the story about that fantastic old car and the conversation you had with the owner!' She paused only for a moment before she continued, eyes alight with enthusiasm. 'And then I'll turn the relationship into a steaming romance so despite you and the car owner having this sarcasm issue between you, you meet up somewhere and kind of realise you're really attracted. Some weird place, I'll have to make up a good location, where you can't get away from each other.'

This is an unbelievable conversation, thought Julia, and clearly fate is signalling that I should tell her more. She made a snap decision to tell Caol what had happened only a couple of days ago in the lift in the City Council building.

'If you can promise to *never* tell anyone who gave you the idea, I'll tell you about what happened when I next met the sarcastic man. But I don't understand how this will fit with your various pseudonyms because this is a very hetero story, and neither of us is gay or trans.' Then she laughed. 'Well, *he* might be, I suppose. How would I know?'

She told the whole long and detailed story of the unwashed, creepy guy and how she knew he was a pervert, how Milton shoved her into the corner in the lift and how they stood staring into each other's eyes outside the lift, so close they were nearly touching. Nothing was left out, not the detail of how her hand had ever so slightly moved towards Milton or how his hand had briefly touched hers or how she had relished the feeling of her hand on his shoulder.

After a slight hesitation she added, 'I very nearly moved my hand and touched his neck. I didn't, of course, but the impulse was so strong, as if I knew the feeling it would give me if I touched his skin. As if I'd done it before.'

When she finished, Carol smiled a happy smile. 'Thank you! I love it! I'm going to write masses of notes about this before I go to bed so I don't forget any of it – it's gold, pure gold. I couldn't have invented a better situation for a romance if I'd tried. And mind you let me know what happens next! A text now and then will do.'

They parted late in the evening after drinking slightly more wine than was good for either of them and eating delicious and very expensive bar snacks. Not until they were leaving did Julia discover that Carol had ordered everything to be put on her room bill, which made Julia feel guilty about how many bar food delicacies she had ordered from the menu.

'For God's sake, don't worry about it,' said Carol. 'This has been the best evening of my trip so far, and you've given me a fabulous backbone for a book. I can't wait to get back to my laptop and start mapping out the plot. I'll probably be up most of the night now.'

She put her hand on Julia's and gave it a little squeeze. 'You've got my phone number now, so first of all text me your e-mail address so I have everything I need to get in touch. Later on, I'll send you the manuscript when it's finished and polished and edited, or whatever my publisher is going to insist on. And then when it's printed I'll send you a copy.'

Julia left her car where it was, hoping there wouldn't be a ticket on it in the morning and took a taxi home. As she once again fished around in her bag for the key to her apartment she realised that something had changed. Talking about the lift episode with someone, who didn't know Milton, and who didn't know her well either, who had no preconceived ideas about any of the things that might influence the story, had been a cathartic experience. And maybe she might be able to use the feeling of being a character in a story to get some distance on her confusing thoughts about Milton and the things that had happened. This feeling might not last, but it might make her internal conflict a little bit easier to tolerate.

She sat on the edge of her bed and sent a WhatsApp message to Barb with the photo she and Carol had taken of themselves before they parted. 'Thank you for lending me Carol, who is a perfectly gorgeous woman, very funny and very clever. I enjoyed tonight more than I've enjoyed a date for a long time. I'll call you tomorrow and tell you the details. J'

20

It wasn't until Saturday that week that Linda moved in. There had been some minor complication with the cast for the leg that had been in traction, but finally just before lunch she arrived in a special van with a lift platform for a wheelchair, with her crutches tucked in on one side and her laptop on her knees with a little bag resting on top of it.

The driver of the van texted Julia from the entrance and she went down to show them up. Both Linda and the driver stared mesmerised at the display playing out on the white glass wall in the lift. When Linda had been installed in an armchair in the living room the van driver left with the hospital wheelchair, closed the door behind him and Linda exclaimed, 'That lift! It's amazing.'

'It is,' said Julia and sat down opposite Linda.

'I never get tired of it and Seb's going to love it – he's seen my video of it. Now, what would you like to do first? We can do a tour of the apartment which isn't terribly big, and I can show you where I've put all your belongings. Or you can sit here and watch me make lunch, and then I'll call Gwyneth, who lives next door, and she'll come and join us for lunch. It's your choice and there's no hurry.'

'What a lovely flat this is,' said Linda instead of replying and looked around the large, airy room. 'I'd been so worried about what was going to happen when I had to leave the hospital or if I'd have to stay there for weeks and weeks. I can't tell you how grateful I am.'

'You've already done that.' Julia laughed. 'As I said to Seb once, saying thanks or apologising once is quite enough, there's no need to repeat it. But I must confess right away that I've taken a liberty with your possessions. I didn't just go and pick them up. The staff at the hostel had put all your stuff into big cardboard boxes, so I unpacked them and put it all away. I know that's an invasion of your privacy, but I thought unpacking and putting things away and hang things in the wardrobe would be so tiresome for you. So, I did what I did.'

'God no, I don't mind at all. I hadn't even thought of how difficult it would be to unpack a whole lot of cardboard boxes, so that's great –

thank you. I think I'd like the tour of the apartment first and then have lunch. And of course, I want to meet Gwyneth. How come she's at home all day? Does she work from home?'

Julia suddenly realised that she hadn't told Linda anything personal about Gwyneth, which seemed a bit bizarre when Gwyneth was going to be Linda's emergency helper in case something went wrong.

'She used to work in the central city library here - she's a trained librarian, and she's way past retirement age, so she doesn't work at all now. But it would be hard to find someone smarter and more with it than Gwyneth. She and I play Scrabble now and then, and she likes a glass of wine, and she's funny, very entertaining. But maybe you should know this about her too - she stays inside nearly all the time. She will go out and do the shopping if she has to, but I often do her grocery shopping for her. Her friends come to visit her, but I've never heard her say she's been to someone else's place apart from mine. I've never asked her why she doesn't like to go out, but it doesn't matter. It's just the way she is, and we all have our little peculiarities.'

Linda nodded and looked interested, but Julia could see she was wondering now what Gwyneth would be like, and perhaps slightly apprehensive at the prospect of interacting with someone so much older.

They did a slow tour of the apartment and Julia showed Linda where things were kept in the kitchen and told her she was under no circumstances to try and lift anything hot out of the oven. When she showed her the toilet seat, Linda immediate sat on it and pronounced it very comfortable. 'Those handles are clever - very clever.'

'I'd never seen anything like it before- they're very practical.' Julia yanked hard on one to demonstrate how securely they were stuck to the wall. 'Now let's go and check out your bedroom.'

'Wow, what a gorgeous room!' Linda stopped just inside the door. 'Much bigger than I thought it would be. Our spare room at home is tiny, but this is lovely, like a little sitting room. Plenty of space to move around.'

Julia opened the wardrobe and showed her the clothes hanging up and pointed at the chest of drawers. 'Your underwear and non-hanging stuff is in the drawers, and I put your books in the bookshelf and as you can see, also all kinds of things that I couldn't think where you might want them. And I've got a spare charging cord we can plug in here so you can have one here and one in the living room to keep your phone and laptop charged. And we'll put Gwyneth's cell phone number in your phone, so you can just text her if you want her to come over.'

Linda leaned her crutches against the bed and

pulled off her sweatshirt. 'Did I tell you about the brace? No? Well, the cast on my traction leg is coming off in a week and I'll have a brace instead, they're making it now.'

'That sounds much better.' Julia looked around and tried to remember is there was anything else she should tell Linda. 'Oh yes, that little table. I put it in the corner so you'll have somewhere to off-load bits and pieces, but if you're going to use it to study we can move it and you can have one of the dining chairs in here.'

Half an hour later and with a chicken pie in the oven warming up for lunch, Gwyneth arrived and within minutes Linda had told her that her mother was originally Welsh and had come to New Zealand after she met Linda 's father in England.

'I've got a great-aunt called Gwyneth who lives in Cardiff,' she said and laughed. 'And now I've kind of got another great-aunt called Gwyneth who lives here. So funny!'

Julia listened to their conversion while she set the table and realised that any worries she'd had about how those two would get on had been unnecessary. Linda was so relaxed and friendly, and Gwyneth seemed to relate to her without effort. There's a nearly sixty years age gap, she thought, and here they are chatting away, how wonderful.

Over lunch they talked about what kind of routine Linda might want to set up and what she might need help with when Julia was at work. When Julia said that she didn't want Linda to try to take showers or do anything complicated when she was alone in the flat, Gwyneth said straight away that all Linda needed to do was send her a text message when she was ready, and she'd come over and sit in the living room until Linda was safely out of the shower.

'I know you've got those homecare people lined up, but I've read about how they're sometimes short-staffed, and nobody comes,' she said. 'And we can't have that. So, you just text me, I'm always at home.'

And how will Linda take this? wondered Julia. Will she find it difficult to have to ask for help? Will she think she's being treated like a child? But no, Linda seemed to be perfectly comfortable with the idea of having Gwyneth as a willing helper, whom she could call on at any time. In Julia's mind the last worry about the neighbourly support arrangement evaporated.

That night when Linda said she was exhausted and ready to go to bed Julia left her to do her own thing after saying she must call out if she needed help. Then she remembered something she had meant to say earlier and added, 'And don't forget that for the time being this is your home, so you're welcome to invite people to come and visit.'

'I'll wait and see,' said Linda. She paused and looked slightly hesitant before she added, 'I hadn't had time to form any real friendships, or hardly any. I got to know a few people quite well, but I haven't seen or heard from them for ages now.'

Julia studied her face for a moment and tried to assess how affected Linda might be by her apparent isolation. Should she treat this lightly and revert to it at a later date when Linda had had time to settle in, or would it be better to make a comment to see if Linda would open up a bit more. The last thing she wanted was to create an impression that she expected Linda to have a lot of friends, or that she would find Linda wanting if she didn't.

'You could always get in touch with some of them again,' she said casually after a moment's thought. 'Invite them to come and see you here. Visiting people in hospital is such an artificial situation, isn't it? Not very comfortable if you don't know them really well. It often feels a bit awkward to start with, so maybe having them over for coffee here would make a difference.'

Linda smiled and seemed quite comfortable. 'Don't worry about it. I'm perfectly fine, and I've never been one of those girls who needs to be part of a crowd, kind of included in a gang of girls. I've mostly hung out with guys on skateboards. It's not important to reconnect with the people from the course right away, but I might try a bit later. I think I'll be fine here, and it's nice to know Gwyneth is next door.'

'And Seb will come and visit regularly. Not only is he dying to see the lift, but he really likes you, and if you don't mind I think you could be very good for him. He's an only child and having you as a kind of temporary, older sister might fill a gap. Plus, you might be able to help him a little when he runs into trouble with his maths homework.'

Suddenly Linda changed the subject with a surprised look on her face, 'I wonder what happened to my skateboard? Did you see it when you picked up my things?'

Julia shook her head. 'It wasn't amongst the things I picked up. When did you last see it?' And then it dawned on her. 'Oh no! I bet it was left at the skate park when you had your accident - do you remember if they put it in the ambulance with you?'

'God, no - I wasn't in any state to notice what was in the ambulance. I was in such pain with my broken legs and my head hurting. I don't think I'd have noticed if there had been a polar bear in there with me. I bet you're right – it got left at the skate park.'

She thought for a moment, looking back in her mind to the time of the accident. 'I mean, think about it. There we were, that girl and I, crumbled up in a pile at the bottom of the half pipe with broken bones and sore heads and bruises, both of us crying.' She shook her head. 'No, I was screaming. Some helpful guy tried to straighten out my legs and nearly killed me. I don't know how long it was until the emergency services turned up, but I wasn't in a fit state to check where my skateboard was. There were masses of kids standing around staring at us, so probably someone picked up my board and took it.'

'Was it a special one?'

'No, not really. I'd had it for about three years. I saved up for a pretty good one and I've serviced it regularly, you know, so the bearings were always OK, and I rotated the wheels, so they'd wear evenly. I'll have to buy a new one.'

ulia was leaning against a tool bench in the workshop discussing a problem with a distorted Austin Healey boot lid with Morgan, wishing she hadn't come into this cold space without putting her jacket on. She often did this during the cold months, went without thinking from her warm office into the large, wide open workshop space where it was impossible to moderate the temperature. The mechanics all had jerseys under the overalls now, and skinny, young Shane had taken to wearing a scarf around his neck.

'I think you should start closing one or two of the roller doors when you're doing jobs that will take a bit of time – it's freezing in here.'

'No,' said Morgan and grinned. 'You know it doesn't work and it would be cold in here anyway even with the wall heaters on. And we've all agreed we'd rather cope with the cold than breathe in too many exhaust fumes.'

'I think we have this conversation every autumn.' Julia crossed her arms to retain some body heat. 'I used to wear a thermal base layer and a fleece top under my overalls when I worked in here, and I still felt cold. But back to the boot lid - did he tell you how this happened?' She ran her hand over the slightly distorted corner of the lid. 'How did it get to be like this in the first place?'

Morgan shook his head at the thought of how careless the owner had been. 'He didn't think, put a suitcase in and then pushed hard and fast to close the lid with his flat hand. He hadn't realised that the suitcase was too high, and he didn't react quickly enough to the resistance, so he forced it. He claims he opened it straight away but that short time with hard pressure was enough to bend it slightly out of shape. What do you think we should do?'

He frowned at how complicated this might get. 'He says he doesn't want to take it to a panel beater – I don't know why. It's the obvious thing to do, isn't it? And this is a 1957 model, so we'd have to go to one of those specialist spare parts suppliers if the whole lid needs to be replaced, not to mention that we might not be able to get the right colour, so it would have to be imported which would probably cost a bomb.'

'He can afford it,' said Julia callously because the owner of the Austin Healey was a well-known businessman, who had several expensive hobbies, of which one was his car collection. 'If it becomes necessary I'll call him and give him a couple of options, but I think we should try to bend it back into shape before we do anything else. There's a slight chance we'd make it worse, and then a new lid is a must, but I remember reading about something like this a couple of years ago. It was Spitfire bonnet, I think, and someone fixed the buckled lid by twisting it slightly. How about you open the lid, cover that corner with a blanket or something to protect the paint work, and then give it a twist. Might be worth trying before we do anything expensive, it might just pop back into shape.'

Morgan nodded. 'OK, I'll do that first and then we can call the guy if it doesn't work and say we have to order a new one. I think he expected that's what would happen. I'll tell you when I'm ready to twist and I'll detach the lid lining first but it might take two pairs of hands. The others are flat out this morning.'

Julia turned to go back to the office and caught a glimpse of a bright turquoise car pulling into the side of the forecourt, where cars waiting to be attended to, were lined up. The Edsel was back!

Her heart made a little leap in her chest at the thought of seeing Milton Parker again. Ever since the episode in the lift her thoughts kept reverting to him, but she had reached no conclusion. He was wildly attractive, but it wasn't his looks that made her feel is if a strong current was pulling her towards him whenever they were in close proximity, and neither was it lust. Though she had to admit that lust was definitely part of this puzzle of conflicting emotions. To feel so strongly attracted to a man, whose sarcastic reaction to her should have been a turn-off, was beyond strange. The conflict between how her body was drawn to him and how off-putting his sarcasm was made the situation impossible to come to grips with. And added to that was the sensation in the lift when he pushed her behind him to protect her, when she ran her hand up his back to his shoulder. The way she had felt his muscles react to the pressure of her hand and how that had made her feel, as if her hand was already familiar with a feel of his shoulder, as if she had done this many times in the past. Then then the strangeness of how they had stood as if frozen staring into each other's eyes, and the way his hand had for a second touched hers. Never had any interaction with a man given her that strange, vivid impression, that she and he had known each other in some past life or distant place. That they had touched and become familiar with each other's bodies.

She dismissed these rapid thoughts flitting through her mind, put on her customer face and made it to the office just as Milton Parker opened the door and entered. The important thing now was to let no trace of what she had just been thinking show on her face, and to avoid reacting to anything he said or any expression he displayed. She would keep things controlled and not refer by a look or a word to the strange little episode when they had stood too close together staring at each other outside the City Council lift. That he had seemed silently mesmerised at the time didn't mean he felt what she did. Maybe he just fancied her, as those thoughts of his clearly demonstrated, so perhaps it was just lust on his side, nothing more. Her own confused emotions went much further and had the potential to become deeply hurtful.

'Hi,' said Milton without smiling, his voice casual, nearly cold. 'I was giving the Edsel a run instead of taking the truck into town, and I realised that when I was here last I never told you the date the warrant of fitness expires. I had a look after my meeting, and it's due in three weeks.'

'Thank you,' said Julia, puzzled by the coolness of his voice and the neutral expression on his face, not what she had expected after the emotionally charged lift episode. 'We already have the details in the database. It links to the vehicle register, so when we enter the plate number the expiry date for the warrant of fitness automatically feeds through to our system. You should get a reminder in a week if it's due in three weeks.'

'Thank you, very efficient system,' was all he said, still without any warmth. 'I'll wait for the reminder and make an appointment then.'

He left her more confused than ever. There had been no smile this time, so no way of knowing if his response had an undertone of sarcasm or not. Julia watched him walk back to his car and wondered what had caused this slightly chilly approach. Had he realised that she was strongly attracted and nearly physically pulled towards him the last time they met, had he decided to avoid encouraging that, or was he also conflicted about what had happened? Could he sense her reaction to his stealth sarcasm, but didn't know what caused it seeing he thought it was hidden?

But as with all her meandering thoughts about Milton, there was no way of reaching any certainty, least of all about her own feelings. She told herself for the hundredth time that she must stop thinking about him. This obsession was out of character and not something she was comfortable with. It would be better for her peace of mind to mentally dismiss him, concentrate on work and simply shut down thoughts about him whenever they popped up in her mind, as she was sure they would continue to do. Watching the Edsel pause at the curb to let traffic go past she gave it a wry smile and went back into the workshop to see how Morgan was getting on with the Austin Healey boot lid.

That evening, when she was putting dishes into the dishwasher after dinner, and Linda was sitting on the sofa with headphones on her head and her laptop on her knees, Julia suddenly remembered what Helen had said the last time they met for drinks. When they made the date Helen had said there was something she wanted to tell Julia, but now she couldn't think of anything in particular that Helen had told her. She clearly recalled what she had said, and how she herself had wondered if something was wrong, health wise or marriage wise, that needed talking about face to face. Julia picked up her phone, went into the bedroom and pulled the door nearly shut behind her before she called Helen.

'Hi,' she said breezily when Helen answered. 'You know what I just remembered? Last time we met you were going to tell me something and I don't think you did. Have I forgotten or did you forget?'

Helen chuckled. 'I decided not to tell you right then, after all. I think I was still a bit shell-shocked, and I decided the news about the kids learning to make dinner once a week would cover it. But I'm a bit more used to it now, so I'll tell you. I'm pregnant.'

'You're what?! Are you kidding?'

'No, I'm not - not kidding I mean, but I'm definitely pregnant, four months. I only just realised about three weeks ago. I've always had very irregular periods, so I overlooked how long it was since I'd had one. But once we got over the surprise we decided we really like the idea, believe it or not. Now that the boys are self-sufficient as far as daily care and maintenance is concerned having a baby seems like quite a nice idea.' She chuckled again. 'You might find this hard to believe, but the boys have taken to it with great enthusiasm. They think it will be fun to have a tiny baby in the house. We're very surprised, I must say – it certainly wasn't the reaction we expected. And listen to this! Craig said that they're nearly adult now and having a baby will be fun and also good practise for when they have their own. Which is a hilarious comment when you consider he's just turned fifteen.'

'Amazing!' exclaimed Julia, amused and

delighted. 'So, you'll be forty-two by the time this baby is born. Have you had a scan?'

'God yes, at my age it's really important to make sure the baby isn't Down syndrome or has some major defect. Not that I'd have an abortion, but you want to know in plenty of time, don't you? And she's fine, absolutely fine - would you like to be her godmother?'

Julie's eyes filled with tears. 'I'd love to. Thank you, that such an honour. I have two godsons, one of them is my nephew, and a goddaughter would be perfect.'

'Oh good,' said Helen cheerfully. 'We'll call her Julia, or maybe Juliet, so we don't always have to explain which one we're talking about.'

'Oh yes, of course. Imagine having to explain you're talking about the baby when you say, "I wonder if Julia's nappy needs changing" – embarrassing!'

They both laughed and talked about other things for a few minutes and then Helen said she had to go to the toilet. 'I already constantly need to pee,' she said cheerfully. 'I don't know why - it's not as if the baby is taking up much room yet. Must be something in my mind, but whatever the reason I've got to go. Bye!'

22

As the days rolled on, life in Julia's apartment developed a new rhythm. Linda was usually still in her room when Julia left for work, either asleep or doing something quietly. After the first week the homecare supervisor called Julia at work.

'I think we can cease our morning visits. The caregivers tell me that Linda has a good sense of balance, she's fit and strong, and we are no longer concerned about her falling. She copes well with the leg still in a cast, and in a day or two she'll have her brace. So, if you feel she's all right to shower on her own we'll be in touch in another week and check how she's getting on. You can call us at any time, and if she needs more support we can discuss it – I know you work fulltime.'

Gwyneth and Linda established their own routine for the hours Julia was at work, and

Gwyneth came and went at various times of the day. She would come over and sit in the living room while Linda had her shower and got dressed, and then stay for a cup of coffee while Linda had breakfast. Julia realised after a week or two that Gwyneth now spent nearly as much time with Linda in Julia's flat as she did in her own. She would come home from work and find Gwyneth and Linda watching something on Netflix or just talking, and sometimes Gwyneth stayed for dinner.

'It's really strange,' said Julia to Barb when she called her from work one day. 'Those two have managed to totally change my life, and I suddenly have a family living with me in my apartment. A couple of months ago, I couldn't have thought of anything more unlikely if I'd tried.'

'Don't you mind?' asked Barb curiously. 'You're so used to having things your own way and you're so tidy. It must be a bit disconcerting to find your whole environment changed. I hope it doesn't get to be too much for you before Linda's well enough to move out.'

'No, it's fine. On weekdays I'm only really with them in the evenings, if Gwyneth is still here and then we do something together. Watch a movie or play Scrabble. At other times Gwyneth is in her own flat when I get home, and Linda spends a lot of time on her bed with her laptop. She's trying to catch up on some of her missed studies, she says she didn't have the motivation or the energy when she was in hospital, but now she feels motivated and keen again. And sometimes I go out and meet friends, of course, and just leave those two to do whatever they feel like doing.' She smiled to herself. 'And my bedroom is big enough to regard as a bedsit. I have an armchair in there and that little round table that mum used to have in the corner of the living room, so I can get away when I want to be alone.'

'Now that the kids have got over Covid we must come for a visit and get to know Linda, and we want to meet Gwyneth too. This key person in your life we'd never heard about until recently.' Barb laughed. 'This is so weird, like a whole new world opening up, like you had a secret life. And the kids are dying to meet Sebastian.'

'Of course, they must meet him – he's here quite often. Prissy drops him off after school every now and again, so he and Linda can do maths together. Sometimes he's still here when I get home and Prissy stays for a glass of wine when she picks him up – sometimes it's his dad who comes. It's hard to believe that from being a strictly one-person environment, my place is more like a general hang-out space now.'

Barb laughed and Julia knew that she and Anthony would be discussing this more than once and probably speculate about how long she would be able to put up with all this activity.

When their call ended Julia sat looking out into the forecourt for a moment, thinking of how surprising her life had turned out. If anyone had suggested to her that she wouldn't resent having a teenager living with her, having her neighbour coming and going at all hours of the day and often sharing her evening meal with both of them instead of reading quietly while she ate, she would never have believed it. Isn't life funny? she thought. We think we know how we're going to react to some new situation and then when it happens it's quite different. If Linda can't get back into the student hostel next year I wouldn't mind her boarding with me.

When she had a drink with Helen that Friday night she had the same conversation she had with Barb, and Helen said much the same things and smiled at the thought of Julia having had to adjust just so many changes. 'But having her board with you next year, I mean potentially. Really? Would you be alright with her living there permanently?'

'I think I would,' said Julia and took a sip of her pink flower infused gin and tonic. 'She's no trouble, not a bit like what I thought it would be like to have a teenager in the house. But she's probably not typical of her age group, I don't think. She's very self-sufficient, and she's a reader which is such a blessing. She probably gets loud music and all that kind of thing out of her system during the day when I'm not there, so our evenings are pretty quiet, the way I like them to be. And she uses her headphones a lot, so maybe that's the music I don't have to listen to.'

She thought for a moment. 'It might become different if she stays with me next year and makes closer friends at the Polytech, but if she does acquire a bunch of friends they'll probably go out together, and she'll spend a lot of time on her skateboard again once her legs have regained their strength.

On a Thursday night in the third week of Linda's stay the doorbell rang not long after Julia got back from work. She was in the bathroom, and Linda went to the door, then Julia heard a man's voice and Linda saying, 'Do you want to come in? She's just in the bathroom.'

She heard the front door close and wondering who it was she quickly washed her hands but stopped amazed in the door to the living room. Stuart stood casually talking to Linda as if he had a right to be there, and the feeling of having had her privacy invaded swamped Julie's mind with anger before she quickly pulled herself together.

'Stuart - what a surprise.' She tried to keep her voice calm and even. 'What can I do for you?'

'I just called in to see how you are, just a

casual visit – hoping for a glass of wine,' said Stuart, as if they had the kind of friendship where they could pop in and out of each other's homes without warning. 'I haven't seen you for a while and I was in the neighbourhood.'

'Well, as you can see I'm perfectly fine. But Linda and I are quite busy tonight, and we need to have our dinner early, so I think it's better that you leave right away.'

She knew that this could go either way and there was no way she wanted Linda involved in a verbal battle between her and Stuart. The best thing would be if he simply left, so there would be no need for explanations. Linda's eyes we're fixed on Julia's face, surprised and slightly alarmed at her tone of voice.

'Ah, well,' he said. 'In that case I'd better leave. I thought you would be pleased to see me again, my treasure. I'll get in touch about a date.'

The smile he directed at Julia was one she knew well. He was baiting her, he wasn't suggesting a date, he was either demanding it, as if he had the right to arrive uninvited, assume he would be welcome and tell her what was going to happen, or he was just trying to upset her.

Impulsively Julia decided that she didn't care if Linda witnessed what would inevitably come next, but she had to say it right now before Stuart left thinking that this was something he could do more than once, turn up on her doorstep unannounced.

'No, Stuart,' she said firmly and looked him straight in the eyes. 'You will *not* come back. You are *not* welcome, we are *not* going on a date, and we have no kind of relationship anymore. We broke it off two years ago and there's no way there is going to be any further contact between us, so would you please leave right now and stay away from me.'

Stuart left with such a casual goodbye that if anyone had heard it they would have assumed he was a close friend leaving. Julia closed the door behind him and turned to Linda, who was now sitting in her usual armchair looking slightly stunned.

'I'm sorry you had to witness that. I had a relationship with him, and he's never got over that I was the one who broke it off. He's the kind of self-centred person, who thinks that if there's going to be any kind of breakup it should be him doing it, and he's never forgiven me.'

'But what if he comes back when I'm here on my own? I don't know if I could stop him coming in.' Linda's face betrayed her anxiety and suddenly Julia realised that this was still a young girl, presumably with little experience of men, however self-possessed she seemed.

'What you must do is check through the peephole in the door before you open it. And if it's him you simply don't open the door, you just ignore it. I had the lock changed after I kicked him out, when he was being a bit too persistent, so he can't let himself in. I'll tell Gwyneth the same thing, so she knows not to open the door to him if he comes when she's here.'

It wasn't till after dinner that the simplest solution struck Julia. 'Of course,' she exclaimed. 'I don't know why I didn't think of that right off. I'll get the building manager to change my PIN code on the keypad downstairs, the one we use if we haven't got our swipe card – each tenant has a different PIN. Stuart must have remembered it, but if it's changed he won't be able to get in at all.'

Linda still looked worried and after a moment she said hesitantly, 'He's not violent is he?'

'No, definitely not. If he was the violent type he would have slammed into me the night I broke up with him. I told him exactly what I thought of him and why I would have nothing to do with him from that day on. Sent him packing with instant effect, he couldn't believe it. He was absolutely furious, but all his abuse was verbal, even when I said that if he didn't leave I'd call the cops and ask them to come and toss him out. Not being violent might be his only good character trait - he hasn't got many.'

'But why did he come now after such a long time?' Linda's face had lost its anxious look and now she was openly curious. Perhaps it was the first time she had witnessed this kind of episode, thought Julia. It wasn't something that happened often in anybody's life, but maybe it was a good thing that she was here. It might have taught her something about life and men that would be useful sometime in the future.

'I think he came because we met up accidentally at an event a few weeks ago, and for some reason his ego prompted him to act in front of my friends as if we had only parted temporarily, as if we'd had a minor disagreement that we could easily get over. He was trying to rile me, one of his favourite pastimes. Which I didn't let him get away with, of course. He's a complex man, self-centred and overly fond of himself and his importance and also controlling. As my friends say, he has an inflated sense of his own importance and what he thinks he's entitled to.'

Now Linda laughed. 'I read a book about a guy like that when I was in hospital. They came round with a trolley of library books, and I borrowed a couple of romances to pass the time. And in one of them the poor heroine was a bit like you - there was this awful man who wouldn't take no for an answer, an evil guy, and he refused to back off.'

'And what happened?' Julia had never read a romance in her life and wondered how true to life they were. 'Did she take him back?'

'Oh no, of course not,' Linda giggled. 'That's not how it works in romance books. No, the hero knocked him down and told him never to come back, and the heroine fell into his arms. That's what happens, that's how it works. First there's always some kind of disagreement or a misunderstanding, and they agonise endlessly about each other, and then some creep or maybe a villain comes on to the woman - and to start with she thinks he's nice, but then he turns out to be a real shit, or her parents have decided she's going to marry him, and then the good guy comes back, and they make up, and it ends happily. That's how it works.'

They both laughed and Julia got up to clear the table, relieved that Linda seemed to feel no further need to talk about Stuart.

Talk about agonising about someone, she said to herself when she was getting ready for bed that night, I probably hold the world record now. Tormenting myself has become an obsession.

ulia was standing beside the long freezer counter in the supermarket near Ben's Bistro where she had stopped on her way home after a quick drink with Helen, who now drank the tonic and left the pink gin to Julia. Tonight, she had laughed when she pointed out that Julia hadn't even noticed at their previous dates that Helen only drank tonic.

'That would have been a give-away that night I was going to tell you about the pregnancy, so I got there early and ordered tonic with a tiny dash of cranberry juice to make it slightly pink.'

When Julia walked back to the supermarket car park from the bistro she decided to take the opportunity to pick up some supplies before she headed home to make dinner. But now she stood at the freezer counter hesitating because she had never bought frozen potato wedges before, and she couldn't remember what Linda had said the box looked like.

She picked up her phone and called her. 'What did you say the colours were on the packets of those frozen potato wedges you like? I can't remember what I'm supposed to look for?'

'It's dark blue with a bit of yellow,' said Linda instantly, 'and it's got a picture of a potato wedge, a lovely golden brown one, in a red circle on the front.'

'They all have pictures of lovely golden brown potato wedges on the front, but the red circle might help me find it. Just hang on while I walk along and have a look in case I need to find a substitute. Oh yes, here they are. I'll buy a big box, I'm sure we'll use them. Should I buy some ice cream too? I didn't check it this morning and I have a feeling you and Gwyneth might have finished it.'

Linda laughed. 'God, I'm such a pest, I forgot to put it on the shopping list. I offered it to her a couple of days ago when we felt we needed a treat, and I'm afraid we ate the lot.'

'Fair enough,' said Julia and smiled. 'If you need a treat, you need a treat - and ice cream fixes most things. I'll pick up a couple of boxes. Bye!'

She looked up and realised that Milton was

standing a short distance away looking as if he wasn't sure whether to proceed towards her or not. Taken by surprise, she stood still and didn't greet him because suddenly her mind was empty of words. After his coolness when she last saw him, the certainty that he had erected a barrier in his mind and shut her out made her mute. Meeting him unexpectedly was a joy to be treasured, and alongside that feeling sat the nearly compelling urge to reach out and touch him, which contrasted strongly with his new reserve, and her mind couldn't process these conflicting factors. For a moment they stayed in place a couple of metres apart without speaking, just looking at each other. Then reality and normal manners reasserted themselves. Milton said, 'Hi Julia', and Julia said, 'Fancy meeting you here.'

But having said a few words changed nothing. They remained standing there looking at each other across the space between their trolleys, as if it was a physical void they couldn't cross. Finally, Milton pulled himself together with a visible effort and proceeded past her without further comment. Julia walked in the other direction staring down into her trolley and wondered what was happening to her, and for that matter, what was also happening to him. They seemed to have developed a strange connection, perhaps against the inclination or both, and now when they met they couldn't quite deal with the situation. And not for the first time she wondered how she could have fallen in love with a man who regarded her as ridiculous, and based on his thought-comments, as a sex object. Had fate devised a special brand of torture just for her? She shook her head and headed for the checkout, determined not to dwell on it, to put it to one side and regard it as an aberration, something not to be taken seriously, but she knew she would fail.

24

The text message from Milton the next day took her by surprise, and she hesitated for a long time before she replied.

Can we meet? We must talk, in private, not at the garage. Milton

In private? Did he feel that pulling sensation too, or had he picked up her reactions when she heard his thoughts? But what could she tell him? Revealing the truth to a man with his tendency to be sarcastic wasn't something she could bear to even think about. This weird phenomenon of his thoughts appearing like spoken words in her mind would never be believed by anyone, particularly not by Milton. In her mind's eye she could see his ironic eyebrow quirking up as she tried to explain, and in his mind she would be labelled unbalanced or delusional, which was not a reputation she could afford.

But an hour later she reconsidered. However hard it would be to sit opposite him and feel that barrier between them, the wall he was now firmly ensconced behind, she must do it. Whatever it was he thought they needed to discuss, she was sure it had nothing to do with how she heard his thoughts. How could he possibly have guessed that she could do that? The very idea of her hearing his thoughts would seem ridiculous to him. It must be about her reaction to his stealth sarcasm, some feeling he got even though he probably wouldn't have guessed how clearly she understood his disdain.

It was, of course, possible that he wanted to talk about this strange sensation which they clearly both felt, the reluctant feeling that something drew them towards each other, like the way they had stood together outside that lift, far closer than the usual social distance measure. Every time she thought of it she recalled the feel of his muscles moving under her hand when she steadied herself on his shoulder to whisper not to get into a fight. The way it felt so familiar, as if she had touched him many times in the past. As if she knew exactly how his muscles would flex under her palm and the feeling of familiar comfort it gave her. And once again, even thinking about it made her feel she might cry.

But she could cope if all she had to do was imply that she simply read his face better than he imagined most people could, that she could see the sarcasm he thought he concealed, and then he would probably stop wondering, and after a short meeting they could part. She would stick to that one thing and make no mention his thought comments or the gravitational attraction force. She replied in the shortest possible way.

How private?

The French Bistro by Churchill Park? 6 pm today or tomorrow.

I'll be there at 6 tonight.

With an effort she pushed thoughts of Milton aside and sent a text message to Linda saying she wouldn't be home until seven or so. She could have made it home to change and still been in time at the bistro, but why would she even think of getting changed? It wasn't as if she wanted to impress him. What a stupid instinct, she told herself, there was no need to change what she had worn at work all day. She knew the bright turquoise shirt suited her particularly well, and last time she wore it Linda had commented on the contrast of the colour with her black hair. For the rest of the afternoon her mind was on a loop, where the same thoughts about what she would say to Milton were endlessly repeated. It interrupted her work to the point where she closed the accounting software to be dealt with another day when she could concentrate.

. . .

She saw him through the window as she approached. He was sitting at the table in the corner reading something on his phone and once again she wished she didn't feel so drawn to him. It would be so much easier to deal with this if he wasn't sexy, she thought, and then she laughed at herself for being silly and went inside.

He got to his feet, walked around her and slid her jacket off her shoulders, then hung it on the back of a chair. The move took her by surprise and for a moment she had a disconcerting feeling he was going to touch her and nearly expected to feel his hands on her shoulders or his arms around her. She took an instinctive step to the side because whatever this discussion would turn out to be about, starting the encounter by touching would set the wrong tone. To her the most important thing now was that they approached this situation as civilised people without any emotional or overly personal components to complicate things.

'What can I get you to drink?' His voice was relaxed and friendly and there was no visible sign of irritation on his face. Despite how many times she had tried to think through what she might say she still didn't know how to explain about his not quite concealed sarcasm, but maybe the right words would come to her once she started. She mentally shook herself and tried to dismiss the feeling that this meeting might have been a serious mistake.

'A glass of red wine, please.'

She watched him walk to the bar, and suddenly she couldn't understand why she had agreed to meet him at all. She must have been mad! The feeling she'd had when he took her jacket, that he had nearly touched her, it had instantly brought back the memory of the episode beside that lift. How they had stood staring at each other, as if he knew without a doubt how close she was to touching him, and how she knew he wanted to touch her. And as she had many times before, she replayed it in her mind. Neither of them had made any overt gesture, but somehow she knew, and he knew too, or he wouldn't have ever so briefly touched her hand. It was the oddest thing, not like anything she had experienced before; the way they had stood there staring at each other and how her hand had reached out to him of its own accord, a strange compelling feeling that had been impossible to resist. This connection between them, how they both seemed to know that the other was about to reach out, was perhaps as strange as her hearing his thoughts. She pushed her thoughts to one side and waited.

By the time he came back with their drinks Julia had tucked her confusion away in the back of her mind and her self-protective instinct was firmly in place to shield her. She couldn't take anything at face value with this man; she must be very careful or she might make a fool of herself. He put a glass of red wine in front of her, and she smiled and thanked him, and hoped she looked calm. Tonight, that chilly barrier from the last time they met wasn't obvious, but he might have decided to mask his feelings for the occasion, to enable them to talk.

For a long moment he said nothing, just studied her face as if he should be able to discover what he wanted to know by just looking at her, and Julia sat silent and waited, knowing that at least to start with the advantage was on her side. He had invited her, he wanted something from her, and he should open the conversation.

'What have you got against me?' he asked finally. His voice was perfectly neutral and betrayed nothing of what he was thinking.

'Nothing at all. What makes you think I have something against you?'

There was that half smile again and the little quirk of his eyebrow.

'Every now and then you give me that killer look of yours,' he said. 'Like you did in a restaurant a few weeks ago, and at the City Council when I was coming towards the lift. I want to know what I've done to make you so hostile. I must admit you hide it well at the garage, but I felt it the first time I came in, even if you didn't show it.'

Talk about hiding things, thought Julia and studied his face, now with two perfectly parallel creases between his slanting eyebrows, you're a fine one to talk. And then for some reason she didn't quite understand, she made an impulsive decision to have it all out in the open right away, to find out if she was right and see how he would react. Getting this cleared up was worth the risk of whatever might follow.

'Mainly it's because of your stealth sarcasm, but I find your comments disconcerting, too.'

He looked silently at her for so long that she began to feel nervous. Why didn't he say something? And why that look of disbelief?

'Stealth sarcasm? And comments?' he asked finally. 'What do you mean by stealth sarcasm?'

This was not going well. Repeating his unspoken comments to his face was out of the question, and now she regretted having mentioned them, because they were just his thoughts and therefore not inappropriate. He had a right to think what he liked in the privacy of his own mind. But she must at least tackle the issue of sarcasm.

'You think I can't see your ... disdain, I suppose you could call it. Perhaps sarcasm isn't the right word. You find me inadequate or ridiculous, and you think it doesn't show on your face.' She paused for a moment and added in the name of fairness. 'Though you did apologise for treating me like an ignorant person based on me being a woman when you brought the Edsel in, I'll give you that.'

'Why do you think I feel disdain? It's a pretty nasty word – it implies superiority and scorn. Which is definitely not what I've ever felt about you.' He still looked perfectly calm.

She took a sip of her wine and kept her eyes on his face over the edge of the glass, but the only thing she could see was puzzlement, as if he was genuinely confused.

'I know you think you can hide it, but I can see it quite clearly,' she said finally. There it was again, that tweak of one eyebrow, and suddenly the explanation dawned on her, and she felt herself blushing with mortification.

'Oh, God, I'm so sorry! I've just figured it out, just this minute. It's your left eyebrow – it makes you look sarcastic, but it's just the way it's ...'

She looked intently at his face, tried to imagine him with curved brows or straight ones that didn't slant upward. 'But you didn't, did you? Mock me, I mean. It's the way your eyebrows have that devilish upward slant, it gives you a sarcastic look.'

'Jesus! What a thing to find out about myself at my age! Of course, I never meant to mock you – why on earth would I do a thing like that?' He thought for a moment and said thoughtfully. 'But I must admit I've wondered what you had against me, that coolness, polite but chilly, it was quite unnerving at times and it's why I asked you to meet me tonight.'

Once again his eyebrow did that quirk again, and impulsively she reached across the little table and touched his temple. He didn't move, didn't even flinch or look surprised when her hand approached his face. He just sat perfectly still as her forefinger came to rest on the outer corner of his eyebrow and then he laughed.

'Really – is that it? This is the most bizarre thing anyone's ever said to me. Could you please explain it a bit further, because I haven't got a clue what you're talking about.'

She couldn't help smiling back and said apologetically, 'I'm sorry – I really am! I shouldn't have touched your face, but you were doing it again. One of your eyebrows does this little upward tweak when you do your half smile, it quirks up at the outer corner and it makes you look sarcastic. But I've just now figured out that it's not sarcasm, it simply goes with that half smile.'

'OK,' he said and raised his glass as if in a toast. 'I wasn't aware of that. I'm glad we've got that sorted out, but I don't think there's anything I can do about it. And would you care to explain those comments you referred to earlier? Another mystery I wasn't aware of. When did I make a comment about you? And to whom?'

Julia looked down at her glass and couldn't think of an answer, the seconds ticked by, but nothing came to her. This was getting to be a very long silence, but she had to get this right. She mentally discarded one explanation after another as impossible to make even remotely credible sounding. If only she hadn't said that word! But once said she couldn't take it back, and she realised from his question that he thought she had been told he had talked about her. Her mistake mortified her coming straight after apologising for touching him and mistaking his quirky eyebrow for sarcasm, so it was imperative to deal with this last issue right away. Backing out now would make her look ridiculous. With a feeling of acute discomfort and a high degree of trepidation about the outcome she finally spoke. 'I knew what you thought.'

'When?'

'When I turned around and gave you that killer look, as you call it, before you got into the lift in the City Council building.'

She saw the second he remembered, now he looked amazed and slightly apprehensive at the same time. 'You know what I thought? Really?'

'About my backside,' she said looking down into her glass, unable to face him. 'At first I thought you'd *said* it – I heard it like spoken words in my head. That's why I gave you that look – in case you *had* said it in a place like that, in front of other people.' She hesitated before she added, 'But then I knew it was a thought I kind of heard inside my head – it's happened before.'

This was the most difficult conversation she had had in her entire life. Her skin was crawling with embarrassment, and she felt sure her face was red. He must think she was crazy, he had to. Nobody normal would ever have said anything so mad.

'It *is* a gorgeous backside, I stand by my opinion,' he said and started to laugh again. 'Christ, Julia! How the hell did you guess what I thought?'

And then he took that thought a step further and stared hard at her. 'But it wasn't just a lucky guess, was it? You said it's happened before. Did you know what I thought in the restaurant? You turned around and gave me the killer look that time too. And how do you know these things?'

All she could do was state the simple but unbelievable sounding truth. 'I just know, don't ask me how. Sometimes I know exactly what you think.'

She paused and considered if this was all she would tell him then added, 'But not all the time. I've picked it up a few times, three or four I think – and it's only when it's about me. And don't ask me how it works, because I don't know, and it's scary when it happens, not *what* you think, but that it happens at all. Like I've turned into a freak or lost my mind.'

Devastated by embarrassment she looked away and wondered if this could possibly get any more awkward, if she should get up and leave right away, but instead of commenting he surprised her by reaching out and curling his fingers around hers.

'Don't look like that! It's not the end of the world, and it's very interesting. I've never heard of anything like it in real life – it's like science fiction. Tell me what I thought in the restaurant and let's check how precisely you get it.'

She found it hard to believe that he seemed to believe her without any fuss, and that he now wanted to test it out, like it was an experiment. It was the last thing she had expected to come from this strange discussion, but she knew she remembered his thought word for word.

She cleared her throat and tried to make her voice neutral, as if having to say this wasn't causing her to inwardly cringe. 'You thought, "that guy is years younger, he looks about twenty and it's not a nephew or something, I can tell he's after her". And I knew you hadn't said it out loud, you were too far away for me to have heard it, but you were looking straight at me when I turned after I heard the words in my head, and you smiled.'

If this was one of those posters they use to teach autistic children what facial expressions mean, his face now had the perfect "totally taken aback" look. She made no comment, just waited.

'Spot on – that's exactly what I thought. Amazing! And he *was* smitten, wasn't he?' said Milton. 'He looked as if he might leap on you there and then – don't forget he was facing me, and I could read his face like a book. The poor guy was consumed by desire. If I smiled it was because the whole situation was so entertaining. He looking as if wanted to grab you and ravish you right there, and you were presumably looking as cool as ever, though I couldn't see your face until you turned around.'

'He's a lovely guy,' said Julia defensively. 'He's a customer, a welder. Right at the start when he first asked me out I told him I'm far too old for him, but I did something really stupid. The third time he asked me I accepted, and then it was hopeless to try to dissuade him from taking it further. So, I broke it off, I just had to before it went too far. He started believing we were going to have a long-term relationship and he would end up hurt when I eventually broke it off.'

She couldn't believe she was telling him all the details like this, not what she had planned when he first asked about Ashton, but she continued. 'I hadn't thought he'd take it seriously, that wasn't what I had expected. Quite the opposite in fact.

I'd thought he would get tired of me after a while and get interested in someone his own age. And then his older brother turned up and said I had to go out with him one more time and tell him properly that it was over and kind of reinforce why, because he still thought he'd be able to talk me into changing my mind.'

'And is it over?'

There was no mistaking that intent look. He wanted to know the whole thing, but should she tell him? Oh, for God's sake, she said to herself, just tell him the whole damn thing, and let him judge her if he felt like it. She had embarrassed herself and disconcerted him already, and this awkward conversation couldn't get any worse, so she might as well give him every detail of the sad Ashton saga.

'Yes, definitely. And before you ask more specific questions – yes, I went to bed with him once. We went out three times, had sex once, and now I've managed to end it. I thought it might be amusing to have an affair with him on and off until he got tired of me, but it wasn't fun - it felt wrong, like I was using him, because I wasn't in love with him. He's so sweet natured and gorgeous looking, and he was so keen, he just wouldn't give up. But we had nothing in common, apart from that basic attraction. And that kind of thing doesn't survive, I don't think, if there's nothing else to bind you together. All our conversations were about meaningless things – meaningless to me, not to him. I was stupid to even start it. Well, I didn't start it, but I let it start, so I'm guilty of bad judgment.'

'OK,' said Milton. 'Two things - do you get anyone else's thought come through like mine did? And how old *is* that young guy?'

It was only then she realised that Milton was still holding her hand, and she tried to twitch it free, but his hand simply clasped hers more firmly. 'Well, are you going to tell me?'

'He's twenty-one or twenty-two. And I've only twice heard anyone else's thoughts apart from yours. One was my sister when she wondered how my involvement with the welder was going and why I hadn't mentioned it, so it was about me, and the other was a woman I met in hospital, and her thought was about me too. It's never happened with anyone else. I think it's something … localised, some kind of weird connection. Like when I'm physically near someone who's temporarily on the same wavelength or something. It's only happened since I got concussed a while ago when a little boy on a scooter knocked me over in Rule Street.'

His hand tightened around hers until it hurt, and his voice was incredulous. '*You* are the woman Seb knocked over! For God's sake – what an incredible coincidence!'

$\mathcal{M}$ ilton and Julia stared at each other for a few moments and neither of them seemed to know what to say next. She wondered if she should ask him to let go of her hand, but now that he had relaxed his grip again it felt nice, so maybe she would let his hand stay there until he removed it of his own accord.

Finally, Milton said, 'Will you have dinner with me – now?'

She only thought for a moment because suddenly and surprisingly she realised that the thing she wanted more than anything was to stay here and continue talking to Milton, however difficult some topics might become.

'I'll have to organise something for Linda, I don't want her heating something and lifting it out of the oven while she's on crutches – well, only one crutch now, but it's still too dangerous. I'll call her.'

And for the second time she made an impulsive decision, and only afterwards did she think how out of character this was and thought it must be something to do with Milton. 'Or we could have dinner at my place, and you can meet Linda – no, I think we need to talk a bit more, just the two of us.'

Once again he was looking incredulous. 'Is that the Linda Seb went to visit? Oh, of course it is, God, this is so weird … of course, it is the same Linda, and you're the woman who took him to the hospital to visit her, and now she's staying with you. I can hardly get my head around this, it's incredible. He thinks you're the most fabulous person he's ever met. Ultra cool, I think was the expression he used. I had dinner at their place last week and he couldn't stop talking about you. He must have mentioned you by name, but it didn't register for some reason.'

'How do you know them?' This coincidence is so strange, she thought, and as he said it's very unlikely to have happened, but it had, and now they had another link, apart from the gravitational pull thing and his thought comments.

'Sebastian's my godson. His dad and I have been good friends for twenty years or more, since we were in our twenties.'

'But Seb said he's named after his godfather – does he have two?'

Milton shook his head. 'My middle name's Sebastian. Prissy didn't want him called Milton.'

Julia slid her hand out of Milton's, picked up her phone and called Linda. 'Hi Linda, I've been asked out for dinner as well as a drink now – would it be ok if I order fast food to be delivered to you? Just tell me what you want, and I'll do it now.'

'Hang on a moment,' said Linda, and Julia heard her talking to someone in the background, then she was back. 'Gwyneth is here - we've been playing Scrabble, and she says she'll order food for us both and we'll eat together. We were just talking about starting this new series on Netflix until you get back – it looks gorgeous, a Korean thing we've been waiting for.' She laughed. 'But if you're going to be out for a bit longer we can probably fit in a couple of episodes or even three, not just one.'

'Oh, good! Tell Gwyneth it's my treat, I'll fix it up with her later. And tell her to get a bottle of wine out, she knows where it's kept. I'll see you both later. Bye!'

They stayed where they were and ordered from the bistro's evening menu which Julia had never tried before. 'Cottage pie!' she exclaimed. 'What an unusual thing to find in a bistro, particularly one run by a Frenchman. I love cottage pie. I can't even remember when I last had it. I must make it one night. I'm trying to educate Linda a bit about real food. Her parents seem to have raised her on a mixture of frozen dinners and ready-made stuff from the deli counter at the supermarket. And it's great that Gwyneth is with her tonight, so she's not alone.'

'I heard her mention Gwyneth – it's an unusual name these days.'

It made Julia smile. 'She's over seventy and from Wales originally, which explains it. She's my neighbour. Did you hear all Linda said?'

'I think so. She's got one of those very clear, light voices, like an instrument. How do those two get on – there's a huge age difference.'

'They're the best of friends, which I hadn't expected. They play Scrabble together and they're both addicted to watching romantic movies and series on Netflix, as you probably heard. Which I never knew Gwyneth did before she got together with Linda, but apparently she's always done it, and they spend hours watching things while I'm at work. And Linda spends a lot of time online when she's alone and not reading, so I've had to add another slice of data to my broadband subscription, she used my month up in a week. All sorts of surprising things are developing in front of my eyes.' She smiled at the memory. 'The other day I came home, and they were watching a video clip on Instagram on Linda's laptop – a clip of Linda skateboarding in the half pipe, and Gwyneth said she's watching a lot of skateboarding on YouTube now, it's so amazingly clever. I showed it to Seb too, and he was very impressed.'

There was a long silence then, while Milton studied her face as if he'd never seen her before, and Julia looked back and thought she had never before felt quite like this. As if someone else's scrutiny was a silent conversation, a wordless exchange with someone she had known forever and trusted totally.

Finally, he said, 'You've created a little community that spans more than sixty years from the youngest to the oldest, if you include Seb which I think you must. He clearly regards himself as part of your created family. You're the most amazing woman I've ever met. A bit like my wife, which is why I married her, but I think you take the top honours.'

Something sudden and frightening happened in Julia's chest while she stared silently at him, unable to respond. She made an effort to pull herself together and process what he had just said without showing how she felt. His wife? He was married! She knew instantly that she mustn't show how she felt now, but neither could she leave. She had to ride this out calmly, so they could part as friends, or she would expose how she felt about him and become an object of pity or embarrassment. How could she have misunderstood his interest to such a degree?

A waiter arrived with their plates and her thoughts raced while she thanked him and watched him fill their wine glasses. Perhaps Milton was just hoping for an affair, and she had imagined too much and made assumptions like a silly teenager.

She lifted her glass and asked as casually as she could manage, hoping her voice wouldn't reveal her inner turmoil, 'And what does your wife do?'

'She's dead,' he said bluntly with a confused expression as if he wasn't sure what she meant. 'Una died four years ago – ovarian cancer that was caught too late. She was a painter and just about to make a real mark in the artworld, I think, but it came to nothing.'

A strange feeling of relief mixed with something else she couldn't define took hold of Julia and she felt her eyes fill with tears. She looked down at her plate and tried to control her emotions before her tears overflowed, but something alerted Milton. 'For God's sake, Julia! What's the matter? You're not about to cry into your cottage pie, are you? Or did you know Una from somewhere? Didn't you know she had died?'

'Sorry – I thought you meant you had a wife now, so I wondered if I was making an absolute idiot of myself. I thought we …' Her voice tapered off and she had no idea what she had meant to say because she could think of nothing that seemed acceptable.

Unexpectedly Milton got to his feet and said, 'Would you stand up, please?'

Much to her own surprise she did what he asked, pushed her chair back and got up.

'Come here.' He pulled her in and held her tight against his chest and she felt his warm breath on her temple when he spoke. 'We do … whatever it was you were going to say a moment ago. I feel it too. I knew it from the first time I saw you. I struggled against it when I didn't understand your reactions, but we definitely do … whatever it is.'

She leaned into him and felt one of his hands slid up through her hair and curve around the back of her head, holding her against his shoulder, then his lips briefly touch her temple. Unable to resist she relaxed fully against him for a moment before she stepped back. 'Thank you – but let's eat before our food gets cold.'

People at other tables were watching them now, leaning together discussing what it might mean. She exchanged a glance with Milton, who just chuckled and sat down, as if nothing of importance had taken place. Suddenly there was a short, angry exclamation in her mind. *Fuck!* and she saw a dark blue flash in front of her eyes. She turned her head and there, on the far side of the room, where she hadn't noticed him, was Stuart and two men. She met his eyes without revealing she had recognised him, let her gaze smoothly continue around the room and smiled at Milton.

This is so weird, thought Julia an hour later, and studied her face in the restroom mirror while she washed her hands. Nothing so surprising and so deeply meaningful had ever happened with a man before. The connection was strong, and they both felt it. Not just physical attraction, something deeper that she couldn't put her finger on, maybe trust was part of it, but she knew it was real. And they both had the ability to call a halt to emotions boiling over and save it for later, to reclaim their composure as if nothing had happened; a great trait to have in common.

26

⸻

few days after Stuart's unexpected visit Linda and Julia were sitting quietly reading in the living room after dinner, and Julia was just thinking of going to bed early and taking her book with her, when Linda looked up.

'You know when that guy came the other day, Stuart - and you said he wasn't violent even though you made him very, very angry when you broke up with him and threw him out. But some people, maybe mostly men, they'll say things like, "I lost my temper because you make me angry, I didn't mean to hit you". But then later on, they do it again. Do you think sometimes it's your fault if you make them angry and they hit you?'

While Linda had been speaking Julia had quickly considered the implications and the potential consequences of entering into this conversation with a teenage girl who was only temporarily in her care. But Linda's expression of genuine query told her that this was important and possibly rooted in something personal, and therefore she must deal with it as best as she could.

'I don't believe anyone has a right to hit or assault someone else even if they have made them angry. Making someone angry is just one of those things that happen in life. You know how it is, sometimes you make someone angry without intending to or you might do it on purpose for some reason, but we're all responsible for our actions. Adults should be able to exercise self-control, reign in their anger or simply walk away until they've calmed down. Like we tell children that hitting isn't acceptable, and that the best way to cope with nearly overwhelming anger is to simply turn around and walk away until they feal calmer.'

'That's what I think too,' said Linda and after thinking for a couple of minutes she spoke again. 'My dad says that to mum, he hits her and then he says how sorry he is, and sometimes he cries and says he'll never do it again and tells her he loves her, but it was because she made him so angry he couldn't help himself. I think it's wrong, and I've told her I think it's wrong and we should stop it – somehow.'

Julia knew that a few wrong words now could turn this into something that wasn't her place to say, but she had to respond with something. Maybe the trick of asking a question instead of commenting would lead her in the right direction. 'What does your mum say when you tell her you think it's wrong and he shouldn't hit her even if he is angry?'

Linda looked sad, as if she was mentally reliving one of those moments with her mother. 'She kind of agrees with him. She says she knows she makes him angry when she argues with him, and it's because she is very clever with words and he isn't, so he ends up not knowing how to respond, and it makes him furious, so he hits her - hard.'

'And can you think of any way to deal with that? Do you think there is any solution that is realistic in a situation like that?'

This was turning into a very interesting conversation, and Julia knew that Linda must have reached a level of total trust to tell her such personal things about her family life. Now it was up to her to deal with it in the right way, which felt like a huge responsibility.

After thinking for a few moments with her gaze on the book in her lap, Linda continued.

'I did think I'd found a way of solving it just before they went away. I told mum if that's how it was, if her clever way of arguing made him so frustrated that he got furious, then maybe she should try to not press him so hard and not argue so cleverly. Maybe *she* could do that thing they tell us to do at school, turn around and walk away and think about it. I don't know if she will, and there is no way I'll ever find out if she tried it of course, not now that they're away for two years or more. I can't ask her in a message, that wouldn't feel right. Maybe I'll ask when I see her next. I hope it will work.'

'You're an amazing girl, Linda - so mature and so understanding, but I think there's more to it than just getting your mother to be less clever with her arguing skills, you know. I think we must keep in mind that self-control needs to be exercised on both sides. Maybe she should stop being so argumentative and possibly nagging, and maybe he should recognise the signs of an argument he's going to lose, recognise that he's losing his temper and simply walk away.'

'I know, it could probably be solved if they agreed on the tactics - I've often kind of imagined it just like that in my mind.' Linda gave her a wry smile. 'I've pictured them at an early stage of one of those dreadful arguments - both of them turning around and walking away in opposite directions leaving an empty space where they stood a few minutes ago. I kind of see it like a film clip in my mind.'

Julia got up and walked around behind the sofa where Linda always sat in the same corner, leaned over to put both her arms around her and kissed the top of her head. 'I'm proud to know you,' she said. 'You're a treasure, and I hope your parents are very proud of you too.'

In bed that night Julia went over their conversation and wondered how many nineteen-year-olds would be able to stand back from family loyalties and the violence happening in front of them and come up with such rational ideas about how her parents could deal with their problems. Not many, she thought, it would be too easy to take sides, to feel more loyal to one parent than the other. But somehow this incredible kid can see it like from a distance, without letting her feelings for either parent get in the way of rationality.

She opened her book and continued reading where she had left off an hour earlier, but her mind was no longer on the story. She turned her light off and lay quietly thinking of what she had said to Helen, that she wouldn't mind having Linda as a border if she needed someone to live with. Their conversations had always been good, but now she felt they could develop a true friendship, very different from just the normal teenager-adult relationship. It already felt as if they had developed the kind of trust and understanding she had with her closest friends, despite the difference in age and experience between Linda and herself. It was like an unexpected gift; to offer help to someone she hardly knew and discover she had acquired a genuine friend.

The next morning Linda got up and set out the breakfast things on the kitchen bench while Julia was having a shower, instead of staying in her room until Julia had left for work.

'You're up early,' said Julia when saw what Linda had done. 'This is a nice - are we having breakfast together today?'

'I think I've been a bit lazy. There are lots of little things I could do around here now that I only need one crutch - and sometimes I just use it as a walking stick. It's time I earned my keep as my granddad used to say when he told me to do some chores for him, and having breakfast together is kind of nice, don't you think?'

'Very nice, a real treat.' Julia smiled. 'But don't get carried away trying to be useful, that's not why you're here. And that's another thing I want to talk to you about. You know how I told you the people at the Polytech said you might have to start your first year again at the beginning of the next academic year because of the amount of time and practical experience you've missed. That *could* mean that you won't get a place in a student hostel, because technically you'll be a second year student then. It sounds ridiculous, but the rules are the rules.'

'I know.' Linda frowned at the toaster and dropped two slices of bread in. 'I was thinking about it the other day. I'll have to find someone to flat with before the long summer break or I'll miss out. All the good flats will be fully booked before the long holidays start. I've heard that people organise themselves into flatmate groups way in advance. The trouble is I don't know enough people to be able to network.' She peered into the toaster and Julia had a feeling she didn't know quite how to continue. 'I'm not quite sure how to go about it. It's not something I'm good at, networking with new people. It's not a skill I ever needed in Westport where I knew everyone.'

She moved to the kitchen window and looked out as she continued. 'I know you think I'm pretty mature for my age, but there are gaps in what I know how to do. Things I've never had to think about before.' She turned to face Julia and the smile on her face was slightly forced. 'But I'm sure I can do it, it's just that I don't know how to start. I'll have to figure it out.'

Julia took the toast when it popped up, put it on their plates and said casually, as if they were having a conversation about something unimportant, 'Well, I've been thinking about it too, and if you want to, and if you think you would be comfortable with it and not too restricted, I would be very happy for you to stay here. I initially thought I'd offer you this until the next academic year starts, because you said you don't want to go to your uncle and aunt in Auckland - and you can't go back to your family home in Westport. You've got to live somewhere for the next half year or more, after all. I'd be very happy to have you, but here's another idea for you to think about, and you don't have to make a decision right now. But you could become my permanent flatmate, if you don't feel you'd rather flat with people your own age - I promise I won't feel rejected if you'd rather not.'

The silence from Linda who had half turned away again while Julia was speaking made her wonder if she had gone too far. Mybe Linda didn't know how to say that she would be more comfortable somewhere else in the company of other students. Then Linda turned towards her with tears running down her face and said with her voice breaking on a sob, 'I'd *love* to, thank you Julia! I really love living here. And it's not just that your apartment is so gorgeous, it just feels like a home, it feels like I have a family.' Then she laughed a bit shakily. 'Don't get me wrong. I don't think of you as a spare mother, but we get along so well, and I feel closer to you than anyone else I've met since I've been in the city. It kind of feels like I've known you forever.'

Julie knew that this could become emotional

in a way that would take time to cope with, so she adopted her practical, no-nonsense voice and reached for the peanut butter jar without looking directly at Linda. 'Great, let's do that then. And we don't really have to do anything, do we? All your stuff is here already, all tidily put away.'

'Possibly, just possibly, my stuff won't stay totally tidy. I hope you realise that.'

They looked at each other and laughed, both aware of the state of Linda's room.

'So long as you shut the door on the mess I don't care. If I can't see it I won't worry about it. Now what are your plans for the immediate future? Anything you need to buy or do in town. Don't forget we have the wheelchair in the car, so getting around is easy.'

'I would like to go to the mall one day, I mean the big mall at Corbley, but I can't do that on my own, so maybe we could do that in the weekend. But for today I'll just do what I do every day - all my little tasks still take longer than usual, so they fill part of the day, and Gwyneth will come over and we'll think of something to do. I saw you'd put the box with my chest set on the shelf in the wardrobe, so I thought I might try to teach her to play chess.'

'So long as you promise you won't try to teach me,' said Julia. 'People have tried to teach me to play chess twice and I've been an utter failure both times. I don't know what it is about my mind, but I'm incapable of keeping track of my pieces and the rules however well people try to explain it.'

'Probably it didn't interest you and you were only learning to please someone,' said Linda kindly. 'It would be a hard game to learn if you didn't really want to.'

27

*A*fter repeatedly telling herself to stop acting and thinking like a lovestruck fool, Julia made a resolution on her way to work. She told herself she wouldn't think of Milton once during the day, she would concentrate on her work and focus on things close at hand instead of tormenting herself, as she had been doing for two days. But she still wondered why he hadn't called or messaged her. Was that strange little episode in the restaurant and that tight hug on the pavement afterwards just general friendliness, or did he mean it when he said that he felt something too? Not that they had defined that "something" in any detail, but at the time she had been sure she knew what he meant, and that he knew what she had nearly said before he asked her to stand up. Perhaps he got cold feet after the event, thought he'd committed himself too far and decided to let things cool off. By the time she drove in behind the workshop she had reached no conclusion, as she had known from the start that she wouldn't.

The day became very busy. Morgan had promised a customer that they could bring a vehicle back that morning to have something additional done and then forgot to put it in the computerised booking system, which created a downstream effect that lasted to the end of the afternoon. Julia was making herself a cup of coffee late in the day, having had no time for

lunch, when a text message pinged on her phone.

Have you got time for dinner tomorrow night? Milton

She didn't need to think, but after her troubled thoughts on the way to work that morning she decided that replying straight away might make her seem too keen in case Milton wasn't as interested as she was, so she put the phone in her pocket and sat down at the table with her cup of coffee. But her mind wandered off on its own path, speculating about where Milton would suggest having dinner, then switched to planning what she might wear. She was definitely acting like a teenager, she told herself, much sillier than Linda would ever be.

Her musings were interrupted by Shane, who

appeared in the doorway. 'I'm not gonna have to be a witness – yay!'

'What? What do you mean?' Julia was completely confused, and Shane laughed and said, 'Oh shit, I think I forgot to tell you, they said I might have to be a witness. That guy who came and talked to me - that detective, what's his name – he called me just now.'

'Bartholomew,' said Julia. 'What did he say?'

'They've got the creepy guy, and they've taken possession of his laptops and his external hard drives - those were the things Rob saw on the floor that he said he didn't know what they were. So, the cops have enough to prosecute him several times over without me helping them out.'

'Were you really worried about that?' Julia felt as if she should have known this and maybe talked to him. 'I had no idea.'

'Well, kind of - I'd rather not be a witness against a guy like that. He could probably flatten me with one blow, so it's great that they won't need me. He'll never know who shopped him.'

'I saw him that day when I went into the City Council to talk about the extensions to the workshop. He tried to chat me up while we were waiting for the lift, but I recognised him straight away from the video - and I'll tell you what Shane. Cleanliness *is* important. Even if I hadn't known who he was from the video, I would never have had anything to do with him because of the way he smelled. That guy doesn't wash his clothes very often – if ever.'

'Gross!' said Shane and left. Julia went back to the office pleased that the interlude with Shane had taken up a bit of time, now she could reply to Milton's text without seeming overly keen.

Dinner sounds great – where?

My place, 4 Woodrow Lane, any time after six.

Only then did it occur to Julia that she should have called the police straight after the lift incident, because she knew Milton's name and he knew the name of the pervert. It seemed incredible that she had overlooked it, and it also showed how overwhelmed she had been by emotional confusion at the time. Literally out of my mind, she thought, in a state I've never experienced before.

That night Gwyneth was at Julia's when she got home, and Linda and Gwyneth talked over each other as they tried to tell her what they had just read online.

'That man you told us about, the one with the laptops in his truck,' said Gwyneth.

'He's been arrested and it's all in the paper how the police are trying to work out where all those toilets are that he put cameras in,' said Linda.

'And they said they want people who can add anything to contact them,' said Gwyneth.

'And they've asked people to check the toilets at their workplaces,' said Linda.

'Thank goodness for that.' Julia put her bag on the hall table. 'I've been reluctant to use restrooms anywhere lately in case I happened to go into one where he'd put a camera. I did use the toilet in the bistro the other night, but I checked the corners for tiny cameras, and I was very modest about the way I lowered myself onto the seat.'

They all laughed, then Gwyneth went home, and Julia remembered to tell Linda that she would be out for dinner the following night.

'Ask Gwyneth over if you like, or someone from the hostel,' she said and started preparing a smoked fish pie with Linda sitting on a stool at the breakfast bar watching her. 'We could order food to be delivered from the pizza place or somewhere if you like – you tell me what you want, and I'll do it. Or there might be enough of this pie left over.'

'Are you going on a date? Is it the same guy you had dinner with before? The night you called and told Gwyneth to get a bottle of wine out – is he gorgeous?'

For some strange reason, this little stream of excited questions was comforting, a very teenage way of reacting and demonstrating that Linda still had the characteristics of a girl. Their conversation the previous night had slightly worried her when she thought about it afterwards and wondered if Linda was used to accepting too much responsibility for her parents' problems. 'Yeah, it's the same guy. I don't know him very well yet, but I like him a lot. And before you ask again, yes, he's *very* good looking.'

I'm not going to say he's a sexy beast, she thought and nearly laughed. Heaven knows that might come out some time in the future when she meets him. And suddenly she remembered that she must avoid mentioning Milton's name because Linda might tell Seb about him, and then the game would be up, and everyone would discuss it and comment, and she wasn't ready for that. This whole Milton thing felt exciting and deeply private, something to treasure without telling anyone else. Maybe after tomorrow night she would feel comfortable talking about him, but for the time being she would rather not.

But Linda seemed to be content with Julia's brief description of Milton and changed the subject. 'Seb is coming over tomorrow after school - they're doing fractions and he says he doesn't understand a single thing about fractions and he doesn't want to, but the teacher says they all have to learn it.' She laughed. 'He was so funny when he told me, very indignant about having to learn something he thinks is totally useless. I'm going to try and turn it into a little game - I thought I might use drawings to see if I can get him to understand how it works.'

She shook her head. 'I think he told himself early on that mathematics is a mystery he'll never get the hang of, and now he actually believes it.'

'I think that's very common,' said Julia and put the pie in the oven. 'Particularly with maths. And if Prissy doesn't pick him up until after I've left for my dinner date, could you remember to tell her that we can take Seb with us to the mall in the weekend if he wants to come? What is it you want to buy?'

'It's not that I want to buy anything. I just love going to that big mall. We don't have anything like that in Westport and it's fun just walking around looking at things - well, this time it'll be fun being pushed around in the wheelchair looking at things. I don't think I want to go there using my crutch and risk getting knocked over seeing how busy that place is in the weekend.'

'Seb will love pushing you in the wheelchair, so let's not deprive him of that pleasure.' Julia grinned. 'He'll probably be disappointed when he discovers it's not an electric wheelchair, so he could ride in it with you, but anything with wheels is probably interesting to someone his age.'

28

When Julia left to go to Milton's place the following evening, she saw Prissy arriving as she drove out of the underground garage. She waved and continued on her way with the GPS set to guide her to Woodrow Lane which she had never heard of before, in an area to the west of town where she knew some big industries were located.

Number four turned out to be an unusual looking house made from several long shipping containers, put together like building blocks with a lot of glass linking them. But building a house right next to that huge sawmill, thought Julia, as she parked on the driveway, what a noisy place to live, wonder if he got the land cheap?

Milton must have been keeping an eye out for her because he opened the front door the moment she arrived on the doorstep. For a moment she stood on the threshold just looking at him, and he met her eyes and didn't move or say anything, then he reached out and pulled him towards him, held her tight and said, '*There* you are,' in a tone of voice that clearly expressed how pleased he was to see her.

'What an amazing house,' said Julia when he let her go. 'I've always wondered what these shipping container houses look like inside. I suppose you need a lot of insulation with metal walls.'

'No more than in a house with external cladding of corrugated steel, like lots of houses have these days. Come in and have a look.'

The main living area was much bigger than she had expected.' Let me guess.' She glanced around the room, estimating size. 'This is three forty-foot containers side by side and opened up to form one huge room, right?'

'Perfect,' said Milton and chuckled. 'I knew you would size it up the minute you walked in. The insulation is a special kind that soundproofs extremely well, and all the windows are triple glazed because the mill runs twenty-four hours a day six days a week. From a noise point of view it's pretty bullet proof.'

'What made you build right next to such a noisy place?'

'That's where I work.' He looked at her with a

slight frown. 'I thought you knew - didn't I give you my card that first time I came in?'

'I don't think I looked properly at it – I was probably distracted by trying to figure out what that sarcastic eyebrow tweak was about. I just entered your name and phone number in our database and threw it in the bin, sorry! So, what's your role at the mill?'

This time he looked at her with a decidedly strange expression before he replied. 'I own it, or most of it. My grandfather started it about eighty years ago, and then my father expanded it and built up a big export trade in cut timber, and when he retired a few years ago and went to live in Queenstown, I took over. It's a private company owned by family. It's not strictly speaking all mine, but I have a majority holding. Some of the family preferred capital to investment income and sold their shares to me.'

Julia felt a smile forming. 'Do you know a guy called Anthony Crombie?'

'Oh yes, of course I know Anthony - do you know him too?

'He's my brother-in-law. He's married to Barb - my youngest sister.'

After a moment of surprised silence Milton burst out laughing. 'This whole saga is so full of unlikely coincidences and convoluted connections - if you wrote about it in a novel no one would believe it could happen in a city of over a million. Too unlikely to be credible. But you know what it means don't you?'

'No, I don't have a clue, what does it mean?'

'I can only think of one thing,' said Milton and took hold of her shoulders. 'It must mean that you and I were meant to be together. Think about it, Seb knocks you over, he's my godson and the son of a close friend, who you now also know - and now you turn out to be the sister-in-law of the contracted engineer who fixes our automation problems as the mill. If you and I become a couple, which I really hope we will, then we can never part. It would upset too many social arrangements and make things so awkward, so even if you decide I'm unbearable you couldn't possibly leave me.'

He looked into her eyes, and she could see how serious he was, he really meant what he was saying. 'When I brought the Edsel in and thought you were just the admin person, remember that?'

'How could I ever forget? So funny!'

'I walked out of your office that day and knew I must have you, make you mine. Too gorgeous and cool for words.'

She choked back a laugh and put her hand flat against his chest. 'For someone who hasn't even kissed me yet, that's an incredible statement to start an evening with.'

'Let's have champagne,' said Milton coolly, not at all disconcerted by her amusement.

'Champagne is always good, and I've got a good French one in the fridge. Was I going too fast for you there? Do you need time to think about it? Us, I mean, not the champagne.'

Now Julie I laughed outright. 'No, I don't think I need to think about it. I seem to have spent most of my waking hours agonising about you for several weeks now, I even dream about you sometimes.' She moved slightly closer within the circle of his arms, unable to resist her body touching his. 'So, unless you turn out to have a bondage fixation or some other unpleasant hobby I can think of nothing I would like better than to be one half of a couple with you. Are you going to get that champagne, or do I have to go and get it out of the fridge myself?'

The meal was far more complex than she had expected from a man unless he was a chef. And as she said to Milton, when she complimented him on his cooking, she was fully aware she was being judgmental based on his gender, but she didn't know a single man who cooked, and it made up for him not realising a woman could be a mechanic. Which in turn made him say that anyone as sexy and well dressed as she had been that memorable day must take it on the chin that people got distracted and underestimated her mechanical skills.

When Milton after dinner asked if she wanted a tour of the house, she nodded. 'Of course, I'd love to see the rest of the house. Will the tour include your bedroom?'

'Would you like to see my bedroom?' asked Milton, as if she hadn't spoken, and he had just thought of this by himself.

'I would love to see your bedroom,' she replied and wondered if she should text Linda and say she'd be out late, but decided she would probably figure it out for herself if Julia wasn't there in the morning.

Several hours later Julia lay at an angle to Milton with her forearms resting on his bare chest and watched his blue eyes glinting through thick black lashes. They had talked about everything under the sun, it was nearly one in the morning, and they still thought of things to ask each other.

'Did you every crash a car?' he asked suddenly after telling her about one of his men running a huge forklift into the side of a truck the previous day. She could tell he expected her to say, of course, she had never crashed a car.

'A couple of times,' she said casually and looked away to one side, as if she was trying to remember. 'No, three times – total write-off the last time, bits of car all over the place.'

His expression was priceless now, and she wished she could grab her phone and take a photo of him. He might never have looked so taken aback in is life as he did in this wonderful moment, even better than when he realised she was the person Seb had collided with.

'What happened?' he asked cautiously after a long moment of silence, probably feeling a need to go carefully in case Julia would be reluctant to describe the accident.

'Oh, I won - just. It was a demolition derby - the first time they'd had the end of season races for men and women mixed, and they surely hadn't expected a woman to win it. I left a trail of parts behind me and just made it over the finish line before one of my front wheels fell off.'

She watched the realisation dawn and continued casually, 'I'd converted an old wreck for the race myself – you know, so it was as safe as possible, which earned me even more street cred.'

'You devil!'

'You walked right into that one.' She laughed and put a fingertip on his nose. 'Are you comfortable with me leaning on you like this?'

'Perfectly comfortable,' said Milton. 'Skin contact it's great - provided it's your skin, of course.'

'I must compliment you on your chest.' She ran one hand down his side. 'I love your chest - it's perfect. Not too flat, not too muscly - very masculine and comfortable to rest on. And no man-boobs, I really don't think they're sexy at all.'

'Thank you - and let me tell you I adore your chest and your girl-boobs.'

They both laughed and Julia rolled off him and lay on her back looking up at the bedroom ceiling, which surprisingly was not white like most ceilings but grey. 'Why is your ceiling not white? I don't think I've ever seen a grey ceiling before.'

'Reflections,' said Milton mysteriously. 'This house is at the top of a long, gentle slope and in the winter when the sun is low late in the afternoon the light streams into this room from the low horizon and reflects off the ceiling onto the bed.'

'And?'

'When Una was resting on the bed, which she often did after her various treatments, she found the reflection irritating, so she'd pull the curtains across, but then she couldn't see the view, which wasn't good. So, I painted the ceiling this particular shade of grey, which dulls down the reflected light just enough.'

'You are such a good man,' said Julia and turned on her side so she could look at his face. 'What a lovely thing to do.'

'Very simple,' was all he said.

Julia left at quarter past six in the morning after very few hours' sleep and all the way home she treasured the memory of the night, of waking with Milton's chest warm and solid against her back and his arm across her middle. We might find there are differences that need to be resolved, she told herself as she drove into the underground parking below her apartment block, we hardly know each other, after all, but we can do it. I think we're both so aware of how special this is, so we'll make it work whatever comes up. Not that I expect anything particularly difficult to crop up. I never felt like this about a man in my life.

She was standing in the kitchen with a mug of coffee, leaning against the kitchen bench and looking dreamily out the window towards the distant mountain ranges that now had thick caps of snow on the high ridges and peaks, when Linda exclaimed from the doorway, 'And what time do you call this? Have you been out all night?' And then she burst out laughing. 'As your mother would have said years ago. So, you had a great time?'

'Fabulous - I am so happy I can't describe it. I do hope you'll like him when you meet him.'

'Move over, please.' Linda reached for a mug and made herself a cup of tea. 'Do you think he'll be living here? I mean, not now but soon?'

'Oh no, he won't want to live here. His house

is right next to a factory he owns and that's where he needs to be, he couldn't live in town. I think it's far more likely that I go and live with him.'

There was a moment of nearly tangible silence and suddenly Julia realised how Linda might interpret this. 'Oh God, I should have this first – I'm not getting rid of the apartment even if I do go and live with him. You can just stay here and maybe have a flatmate or two– or perhaps you'd prefer to have the place to yourself. No need to decide right now, but you're not going to be homeless.'

Linda put her mug down and turned to face her, very serious. 'I don't know what I ever did to deserve a friend like you! But you mustn't feel you have to look after me long-term, I'm sure I'll be able to sort things out for myself when I'm fully mobile again.'

'But I want to,' said Julia simply. 'I really do, so please let me. You started out as a project and now I feel as if you're a forever-part of my life, so it's all good.'

And in the undemonstrative way they had already established as their way of communicating, Linda briefly toucher Julia's arm, they smiled at each other and talked no more about it.

When Julia went to get dressed she reflected on how unexpected this was, that somehow her bond with Linda was now so strong that she felt she had an ongoing responsibility for her happiness and security. For the first time in her life, she imagined she truly understood how parents feel. The constant background awareness of how things affect their children, and how it influences how you think and plan. She didn't feel this kind of responsibility for any of her friends her own age or for her sisters; this was a completely new experience. And how had it happened so fast? she wondered, still immersed in her thoughts as she drove to work. How had this built so quickly? This feeling that Linda was her responsibility and everything that happened to her would affect Julia too. Maybe it was that frank talk about her parents, the way her maturity and her search for solutions demonstrated what a special girl she was. Or perhaps it was just that they had similar instincts, their sense of humour meshed, and it had resulted in this indefinable thing called a connection.

29

The following day was the first Saturday for three weeks with sunshine, something that seemed to have been reserved for workdays, and Julia declared it to be the perfect day for going to the mall. They picked up Seb on the way with strict instructions from his mother not to race the wheelchair at dangerous speeds, something he and Linda couldn't stop giggling about as they drove away.

'As if I would,' said Seb, indignant at first. 'I'm not an idiot. Would I do something dangerous and break your legs again?'

'Of course, you wouldn't, we have total confidence in you,' said Julia and listened amused to Linda and Seb discussing where the best ice creams could be found in the mall, and where they would go first. She had to do two circuits at the mall parking lot before she found a sport where she felt unloading the wheelchair and getting it set up wouldn't risk them getting hit by some impatient shopper.

'This place it's one of the worst places I know to go to in a weekend,' she said and braked to let an impatient woman sweep in front of her. 'And I had no idea they don't have enough wheelchair parks. I hope you realise how spoilt you are being taken here by someone who's not a born shopper and who doesn't like crowds. This place always seems to be full of people who've left their manners behind and can't wait a moment longer to spend their money.'

'I think people just take those special wheelchair parks even if they aren't handicapped. They do at the supermarket in Westport. But I've only been here a few times and I just love the place.' Linda laughed. 'And I would have thought you *would* be a born shopper. You always look so smart, and you have some gorgeous clothes.'

'I don't buy a lot of clothes, though, and then I keep them for years and years. The jacket I'm wearing now is probably twelve or even fifteen years old – buy quality and keep it, that's my mantra. I bought it a second-hand shop that specialises in good clothes.'

Eventually they made it safely into the mall's eastern wing and Julia handed the wheelchair over to Seb to push.

'OK - I've got my phone and Linda has hers,

so if we can't find each other we can call and describe where we are and arrange a meeting place. I hardly ever come here, and I don't know where the best place would be to meet. Isn't there a central place in the middle of all these wings? I think I remember it from last time I was here.'

'You mean the rotunda - there are cafes there and fast food places, so that's a good place to meet,' said Linda. 'The cafe with the little round tables is a bit less popular than the other one, I think. I noticed last time I was here, so maybe we should meet there – it's next to the pizza place. There might be more room for the wheelchair there.'

'OK, in that case you two can go off and do whatever you like, and I'll wander around and try and amuse myself, and then we'll meet at the cafe in two hours for lunch. I'm sure you'll have much more fun without me hanging around. How much money have you got?'

It turned out that Seb had taken twenty dollars from his savings and Linda had her cash card, and as she said, she hadn't spent any money for weeks, so she had enough. 'Not that I plan to any shopping. I don't really need anything, but it's always good to know you've got money.'

As Julia walked away in a random direction having no idea where she was going, her phone pinged with a text message, and she stopped to look. It was Milton asking if she had time for a coffee, so rather than explain in a text where she was and why, she called him.

'I'm in the Corbley mall with Seb and Linda.' She moved sideways until she was just beside a wall and put a finger in her free ear. 'And I can't invite you to join us here. I don't think I'm ready to reveal us as a couple to Seb just yet, and I haven't told Linda your name either in case she tells him. I think it would be more fun to do it when the whole lot of them are in one place – I mean Seb and his parents and get a group reaction. Or what do you think?'

'Absolutely. And think of the surprise next time they ask me over for a coffee – if you and I walk in together, and maybe Linda too. Great fun, but can we get together after the mall excursion?'

'I'll come over tonight, after dinner. Seb is spending the day with Linda and I'm dropping him home after dinner, so I can just continue to your place.'

'I had to go to the supermarket this morning, so I got you a toothbrush, a bright red one.' Milton chuckled. 'You know how you said you hate not being able to clean your teeth before going to sleep? Well, you'll be able to now.'

. . .

Julia hadn't anticipated buying anything and she had never regarded herself as an impulse shopper, but after a couple of hours, and much to her own surprise, she found herself sitting at a little round table in the rotunda with three shopping bags on the floor beside her chair. When Seb and Linda turned up Seb immediately spotted the bags.

'I thought you said you never go to the mall because you're a terrible shopper and look at this - *three* bags!'

'I had to do something, didn't I? I couldn't just wander around empty handed in this place where everyone is carrying parcels and bags. I stood out like a sore toe. People were pointing at me, and I could hear them saying, look at that crazy woman she hasn't bought a single thing.'

Seb giggled as he manoeuvred the wheelchair as close to the table as it would go and sat down beside Linda. 'So, what did you buy? Can we see?'

'Let's start with the least exciting thing first.' Julia picked up the biggest bag and pulled out a large square cushion. 'For the sofa in the living room – Linda's spending a lot of time sitting at an angle in the corner with one leg up and it doesn't look comfortable, so I thought we'd have a really large, squishy cushion. If it doesn't fit there we'll put it somewhere else. And then this.'

The second bag she lifted was black and shiny with braided cord handles. She laid it on its side on her knees and carefully slid out something wrapped in tissue paper. 'This is a new dress. I haven't bought a new dress for at least five years, not a real party dress, I mean. I saw this one through the window of what turned out to be a very expensive shop.'

And if she didn't have Milton to show off for she wouldn't have bought it. She smiled at the thought, unwrapped the tissue paper and held it up, but Linda said immediately, 'That's not going to work. You'll have to stand up and hold it up in front of you, so we can see it properly.'

To the amusement of people at the surrounding tables Julia got to her feet and held the bright red silky dress up against her and turned from side to side.

'You look amazing,' said Seb with rapt attention. 'Like a film star. I hope you let me see you wearing that sometime - I'll borrow mum's phone and take a photo of you.'

'If you don't get the opportunity I'll do it,' said Linda. 'Fabulous dress! Bet your new man will practically fall to his knees when he sees you in that.'

Seb looked from Linda to Julia and back again with a suspicious look on his face. 'What new man? Like a boyfriend? Have you?'

'Brand new,' said Linda and grinned. 'She stayed out all night a couple of days ago.'

'That's enough,' Julia wagged her finger at

them. 'Don't tell the whole world what I'm up to, there's already a lot of attention on me now after I did my act with the red dress.'

She bundled up the dress and stuffed it back in the bag with the crumpled up tissue paper on top and just then, before Seb had time to ask what was in the third bag, her phone buzzed with a call.

'Hi,' said Prissy. 'Are you lot in the mall still?'

'We're just about to have lunch in one of the cafes. Do you want us to pick something up?'

'No, but could you ask Seb to keep an eye out for Jonathan, his friend from school. His mum called just now and said the neighbour saw him get into a car with what she thought was an older boy - a teenager. Jonathan had been nagging about going to the mall and she wondered if maybe someone offered him a ride. Not that she knows who this teenager might be, but she's very worried and she's called the cops. So please ask Seb to keep an eye out just in case you spot him if that's where he is.'

'Of course. We'll have our lunch and watch all the people who walk through the central rotunda place, which is where we are at the moment, and then we'll stroll around the other wings and have a look there as well. Has this kid got a phone?'

'No, he doesn't and neither does Seb. I think I might get him one and put one of those tracking apps on it. This has really brought it home to me how helpless you are if a kid wanders off or disappears for some reason.'

They didn't spot Jonathan either in the rotunda or on their wanders through the mall after lunch, but as they headed for the car park at the end of the afternoon Prissy texted and said Jonathan was back home, safe and sound.

'I bet I know who he went off with,' said Seb when he heard that Jonathan was safe. 'He's on the soccer team and the guy, who helps the coach sometimes, he lives down the road from Jonathan, just a couple of houses away. I bet he asked him for a ride. He's got a cool car with a wing on the back.'

Linda turned in the front seat and looked at Seb. 'I hope you'd never do that – imagine how terrified his mum must have been. You know about stranger danger, don't you?'

'Of course – we talk about it at school when we do personal safety and responsibility,' said Seb without batting an eyelid. 'I'd never get into a car with a stranger, not even a woman stranger.'

Julia laughed. 'Personal safety and responsibility? Is that a new subject? We were just told to look out when we crossed the road and to wear out bicycle helmets. And maybe not to go off with strangers, I can't remember.'

As usual the trip in the lift had Seb

mesmerised and silent, and Linda and Julia looked at each other and smiled. As soon as they were in the apartment, Linda held out the little parcel Julia thought was something she had bought for herself.

'This is for you, just a little thank you present. We must talk about me paying you as a boarder, but we saw this and I wanted you to have it.'

'Open it!' said Seb. 'Open it right away, it's a lovely present, we chose it together in a really smart shop.'

Inside the little white box was a pair of dangly earrings in gold and red enamel, and Julia went straight to the hall mirror and put them on. 'Perfect to wear with my new dress! Thank you!'

'I nearly laughed when you showed us the dress.' Linda grinned. 'Like we had communicated remotely somehow – you bought the red dress and we decided these would be lovely with your dark hair.'

I can't mention the red toothbrush, thought Julia, but how strange and amazing, three things today coming together linked by a colour, and then she smiled, red was also the colour that accompanied Milton's thought comments in her mind.

When Julia emptied the third shopping bag in the privacy of her bedroom she wondered what excuse she could have made if Seb had remembered to ask what was in it. She admired the lacy panties and bra she had bought in the luxury lingerie shop in the same red as the new dress, tucked them into her underwear drawer and smiled at the thought of Milton one day peeling her out of the red dress.

30

On the way to drop Seb off before she continued to Milton's place, Julia remembered something she had meant to tell him.

'I asked my sister if her kids could come with us to the mall,' she said. 'I do want you to meet them, but she said taking three kids and a wheelchair to the mall on a busy Saturday would be a nightmare and they had already made a date to go to the early movies with friends. But you'll meet them soon – you and James are nearly the same age and Debbie is three years younger.' Then she laughed and said jokingly, 'Just about the right age gap for you to marry her. Wouldn't that be nice, if all my favourite kids got connected?'

It was only with a nearly superhuman effort that she controlled her urge to laugh when Seb replied quite seriously, 'I think I'd like to marry Linda when I grow up, unless she falls in love with somebody else. I know she's a bit old for me, but I don't really care. Once we're both grown-ups no one will notice.'

'That's a good plan. And she's very fond of you too, she thinks you are so cute and clever.'

Seb frowned. 'It's cute enough to get married? Is that what girls want?'

'Different girls want different things,' said Julia and hoped she managed to keep a straight face. 'But cute is good, good looks and kindness are good qualities too, and you're have both. But I think the best thing of all is being friends because then you'll get on and be able to sort out problems together. I think being good friends is nearly as important as falling in love with someone.'

'You are so sensible. I like talking to you. And do you know what? My mum is going to be so surprised I didn't buy anything at the mall. But Linda and I had such fun just looking at things and talking – I didn't even notice I hadn't bought anything until we were leaving.'

She dropped him at the gate and watched until the front door opened and Prissy waved, before she continued across town and out the other side to Woodrow Lane. To Julia's surprise Milton had either heard her coming or been watching for her car again, because the moment she arrived at the front door it opened, and he did exactly what he had done the first time she came. He reached out and pulled her into a hug and said, '*There* you are!' which made her smile; as if he hadn't seen her for months.

They sat in front of the fire with glasses of wine and Julia thought how odd it was that she hadn't noticed there was a fireplace the first time she came. She must have been so focused on Milton that some details didn't register.

'And how was the big mall?' asked Milton. 'I know you said you don't like shopping, but I suppose the kids had fun.'

'I went into three shops and bought three things, so my shopping record has improved a lot. I left Seb and Linda to their own devices. I thought they'd have more fun on their own. I wasn't planning to buy anything, but I saw something through a shop window that I just had to go in and look closer at – and I bought. And then again in two other shops. A personal best shopping record for me.'

Milton turned sideways on the sofa and studied her face. 'What's that naughty smile about? Are you having secrets now?'

'Oh no, not at all.' Julia smiled. 'I'm just amused at myself for doing any shopping at all, it's not my forte. Quite impressive shopping too.

I spent a lot of money. Totally unplanned, but perhaps it's the best way to shop.'

'And what did you buy?'

Perhaps she would tease him a bit, give him a hint and then refuse to tell him more, he was a man who enjoyed being teased. 'I bought one very large cushion for Linda to have in her sofa corner and a couple of things for me that you might enjoy. I'll show you one day when we get dressed up for somewhere special.'

She gave him a smug smile because she could see how curious he was now. 'And don't ask because there's no way I'm going to describe what I bought, it's got to be seen. I think you'll find it has pretty high impact visually, and if I try to describe it would just ruin the effect when you finally get to see it.'

'OK, we'll have to invent a special occasion soon then, because I have a feeling I'm going to enjoy whatever it was you bought. Or maybe we could have a party to introduce ourselves as a couple to our friends – what do you think? Let them all find out at the same time.'

'A party where and for how many?' asked Julia, whose apartment was not big enough for a large party. 'Do you mean a party in a restaurant or a medium sized party at my place or a bigger party here?'

'Definitely a party here, I think. Seb and his parents haven't been here for a couple of years because I always seem to go to their place, and Anthony knows where I live, of course, but he's never been inside the house. So, for him and your sister and their kids it would all be new. I think it would be nice having it here, something nobody had expected me to do.'

An hour later, after quietly talking and drinking wine until the fire started dying down, they went to the bedroom, where Milton sat down on the end of the bed instead of getting undressed and said, 'Do you mind if I watch you? I've fantasized about watching you get undressed since the first time I saw you.'

Julia's mind played back the scene and gave him an incredulous look. 'And there I was, standing behind the counter watching you leave and wondering why you gave me that little sarcastic smile – if only I had known!'

'You probably wouldn't have liked what I thought,' said Milton. 'Not at that stage. You needed to get to know me first, to trust I really wanted you and wasn't just some sex crazed guy. After the second time, I walked out totally impressed, you were so cool and different. I decided I wanted nothing in the world more than I wanted you. You're beautiful, but it's not just that. It's the whole package, personality and looks, and kindness.' He smiled. 'It's hard to believe you're mine.'

Julia unbuttoned her turquoise shirt and let it fall to the floor. 'Don't worry, I could listen to flattery forever and it's been a long time since I felt like this, so happy and so safe somehow, it feels as if nothing could hurt me when I'm with you.'

She unhooked her bra and slid it off her arms to join the shirt on the floor at her feet. 'I knew it the minute you pushed me into the corner in that lift. That with you in front of me I was safe from anything.'

She shook her head as if she couldn't quite believe what she had just said, unzipped her jeans and stepped out of them. 'And I'm not a woman who needs a man to feel safe. I've always felt pretty confident in my own ability to get rid of unwanted attention - or even physically defend myself, but somehow with you it's all different.'

Her panties followed then jeans and Milton smiled, got up from the bed and started unbuttoning his shirt. 'I know. It is different for me too. I've never felt quite like this before either.'

He unzipped and peeled off his jeans. 'I knew it in the lift when you ran your hand up my back and whispered not to get into a fight. It felt as if we've known each other in some previous life or some other place, as if we were already so close that even your touch was familiar.'

With his boxers on the floor, he walked towards her, and she put her arms around him and rubber herself against him, felt her nipples harden and his body react to her. 'That's exactly what I was thinking later, after we parted that day, exactly that. And then we had that horrid little meeting at the garage when you called in about the warrant of fitness date and you were so cold, so locked away somehow - and it made me miserable.'

'Self-protection,' said Milton and ran his hands down her sides to grasp her bottom and lift her slightly against him, and the intense current of desire made her nearly dizzy. She kissed his neck and spoke with her lips touching his skin and felt him tremble. 'I just couldn't work out what was going on. And our impasse by the freezer counter in the supermarket didn't make it any better. I thought it was all one-sided, just me imagining things, but at the same time I could nearly feel how close you were to touching me, more than once - it was very confusing.'

Without letting go of her he walked her backwards towards the bed. 'That's why I sent you that text and said we needed to talk. I knew we had to sort it out one way or the other or I'd never be able to stop dwelling on it, which isn't like me. I'm not a dweller, so to speak.'

And in Julia's mind one of Milton's thoughts took the shape of spoken words and a strong wash of burgundy red flowed in front of her eyes for a fraction of a second. She looked up at him and said, 'And I love you too.'

For a brief moment he looked confused, then he laughed. 'Aha - another of my thoughts appeared in your head just then, did it?' He turned sideways beside the bed and tilted them both onto it, still clasped together. 'Should I start worrying about it?'

Julia rolled them over until he was lying on top of her. 'No, don't worry - you must have had lots of thoughts about me since the last one that popped up, thoughts I haven't heard at all.' She held his face between her hands and looked into his eyes. 'Do you think we're the only people who do this?'

'Have sex – or talk?'

'Strip and get on the bed naked and carry on a rational conversation at the same time.'

A few days later, after some quite convoluted discussions, Julia and Milton came up with a format for the party which satisfied both their wishes, and during the process of discussing back and forth what form the party would take, and how to ensure the surprise was as effective as possible, they discovered how well they worked together.

'Great, that's all sorted then.' Milton and sank back into his armchair with a relieved sigh. 'We had so many ideas about this event and how to manage to surprise everyone – it got quite tricky, but I think we've cracked it now. And no arguments or ultimatums or sulks.'

Julia stared at him from where she stood in front of the fire with the heat rising up her back making her feel cosy in the way only a real fire could.

'Arguments and sulks? Ultimatums? I can't believe it! Did you think I'd argue and sulk?'

'No, of course not. You're not the type. I was thinking of my past, but let's disregard that. You and I handle things the same way, I think – well, I knew that immediately when I hugged you in the bar. The way we switched from emotional to rational without discussion.'

Julia had to laugh at this brief summary. 'I know. Just what I thought at the time. And thanks for giving in on a couple of things. I know you're not as focused on the element of surprise as I am, so here's a deal. Having put you through that intense discussion I'm very happy for you to make all the decisions about food and drink, and I won't debate about anything. You say you like cooking and I'm only too pleased to avoid it.'

Then she laughed and raised her wine glass in a toast. 'But congratulations on being so close-lipped about your family, not to say nearly secretive. I mean, four sisters! And not a word about them when I had told you all about my two sisters and various things about my past. Not one single word!'

'I just didn't think about it. They are all so much older than I am, and only one lives locally, but I must admit I should probably have mentioned them earlier. It's just that being the youngest, and born twelve years after the next youngest, the age difference has always been a barrier to feeling as we're the same generation. The two oldest are more than twenty years older than I am.' He thought for a moment before he added, 'In practice I was an only child from the age of six. My oldest nephew was born the same year I was – he only missed out on having an uncle younger than himself by a few weeks. I love you in that colour, what do you call it?'

Julia smiled fondly at Milton, who had just revealed something he didn't know for the first time. 'It's called turquoise, but you can call it a funny greenish blue if you like. I'm glad you like it – it's my favourite shirt at the moment, I wash it and put it straight back on again.'

On Sunday morning Milton called Prissy and casually asked if they were free to come for dinner on the Saturday, saying he felt guilty about how many meals he had had at their place since Una died and how lazy he had been.

'I'm inviting another family with kids too, but if they can't come we might have to make it the weekend after, but I'll let you know. And don't bring anything, please, you know I like cooking,' he added before ending the call.

Next he called Anthony with his phone on speaker and invited him and Barb and the children, saying he felt it was time he got to know the whole family and there would be other kids present, so it was a casual get-together. Julia, who was sitting at the breakfast counter drinking coffee and eating toast tried not to laugh as she listened to the Milton's conversation with her brother-in-law. She tried to imagine how surprised he would be if he could see her sitting there in Milton's house dressed in panties and one of Milton's T-shirts with a piece of peanut butter toast in her hand. She must remember to tell him at some later date.

As soon as she had swallowed the last mouthful she called Helen and issued her carefully thought out invitation.

'It's at a friend's place,' she said, trying hard to sound casual and avoided meeting Milton's eyes gleaming with laughter. 'They're having a party for some other families with kids, and I asked if I could invite you. I know you've been a fan of extreme architecture since we were at high school, and you've got to see the house where the party is – stunning! The most way-out design I've ever seen in real life. It's a casual dinner, no need to bring anything.'

She put her phone down. 'Phew! I was hoping she wouldn't go into full third degree mode like she often does because then it's very, very hard to avoid giving too much away. If I hadn't diverted her attention by raving about the house she would have started digging into how the host is and all that.'

Before Milton even had time to respond Julia's phone pinged with a text. 'Right!' she said. 'What did I tell you? This is from Helen, asking for details about who you are. She says, 'it feels strange to just have an address and no name' – I'll just say it's a family called Parker I've become friends with, customers at the garage.'

32

On Saturday morning Julia texted Milton: *Remember Linda knows nothing about the connection between you and Seb so don't say anything to give the game away please. We'll be at your place at three.*

'Here is how it's going to work,' she said to Linda when they sat down for lunch. 'I'll take my good clothes with me and go dressed in jeans and a sweatshirt, so I can help with the preparations and then I'll change before the others arrive.'

'Are you going to wear your new red dress? A bet you are.' Linda gave her a sly look. 'If I'm finally going to meet this new man *and* he's invited other people - it's a bit special isn't it?'

'I think I might wear the red dress,' said Julia, who had already decided that this was the perfect occasion to wear the stunning dress. She couldn't imagine another time when she would ever have such a momentous thing to announce, and such a fabulous opportunity to surprise them all. This party and the red dress were a match made in heaven.

'What do you think I should wear?' Linda looked thoughtful and slightly concerned. 'I don't have anything very dressy. Or perhaps nobody else will dress up.'

'I don't think they will. They've been invited to a casual dinner - an evening with several kids around, not meaning you, so they'll probably come looking quite ordinary. But if you do want to put on something special I remember a dress I hung up in the wardrobe when I unpacked your things - a very pretty, pale green dress. I know it's a summer dress, but if I remember rightly it had little sleeves, and the house is warm anyway, so you won't feel cold inside.'

'Does Gwyneth know?' asked Linda suddenly. 'I mean, that you'll be living with what's his name now? Which I suppose you're going to. You've got to tell her first, she'll miss you.'

'I already told her. When you were studying in your room a couple of nights ago I popped in and told her what was happening.' Julia grinned. 'And guess what she said! Now she has you next door she's it will be more or less the same, and so long as I come back now and then for a game of

Scrabble and a glass of wine, she thinks it's going to be fine.'

Early afternoon Linda and Julia arrived at Woodrow Lane and had only just got inside the front door when a heavy shower of rain pelted down, the temperature dropped instantly, and Milton shut the door fast.

'Perfect timing.' Linda laughed. 'If we'd arrived one minute later we would have got drenched getting out of the car.'

Milton looked at Linda standing there smiling, tall and straight with one crutch casually held in her hand. 'Nice to meet you Linda, and welcome! I'm Milton. No wheelchair today?'

'No, that was just for the mall – I'm fine with just one crutch for balance now, just a safety thing.' Linda studied him for a moment, looked him up and down, and as usual he waited, silent and still, a characteristic Julia had become very familiar with.

'Do I pass?' he asked finally, and Linda giggled and blushed. 'Totally! Sorry, I stared, but you're exactly as Julia said. I hope you've left some jobs for us to do.'

'We brought our party clothes.' Julia gestured at the bag beside her feet. 'And our PJs. We're in jeans, so we can help you in the kitchen or whatever needs doing. Peeling potatoes? Chopping firewood? We're ready for anything.'

'Julia, really?' Milton pulled her close to his side and kissed her temple. 'Chopping firewood? Do you remember what the factory next door is?'

'Sawmill! Right – no firewood chopping then. Linda and I will put our stuff away and come back to be kitchenhands instead.'

The quick tour of Milton's house had Linda wide-eyed with surprise and admiration. 'It's amazing,' she said when Julia showed her the guest room, where she would spend the night. 'Totally awesome. I've never seen a house like this before.'

'I'd never been in one like this either. Milton's bedroom is through that glass-walled passage beside this room.' Julia pointed. 'There's a bathroom through that door there which is for your use. He's only got one spare room and it's totally yours.' Then she laughed. 'And even more amazing, he says if he needs another room at any time he's got building consent to put a container crosswise on top of the kitchen.'

They hung their dresses in the guest room wardrobe and continued to Milton's bedroom.

'Wow – what a gorgeous view! When we drove in I didn't think there would be a view, I didn't realise how much the ground slopes away behind the factory. Let's go and help now. Are you going to tell me who these other mystery guests are?'

'Nope. You'll have to wait until tonight like everybody else. This is a surprise party from many points of view, and I'm not telling you anything.' Then she laughed. 'But you're the only person who knows about Milton. Nobody else even knows I'm in a new relationship, I haven't told a single person.'

'I feel very special.' Linda looked serious. 'I can tell he's a lovely man. I think it's the way his eyes twinkle, you can see he's fun – and kind.'

Linda and Julia nearly immediately found themselves superfluous in the kitchen where Milton seemed to prefer organising things himself, so they resorted to setting up the dining table for the buffet dinner. After a while Linda stood back and studied the scene.

'How many are coming? I mean, how many are going to try and walk around the table and reach everything? I can see the table has those extra bits that you can pull out at each end. Don't you think we should pull at least one of them out?'

'Fifteen, I think. Yes, let's pull out the extension at this end. Did I hear Milton say something about the sideboard, something about the wine and glasses?'

'He said we'll find glasses of various kinds in the sideboard, and we could put them on top, and there's a nice tray in the kitchen for the wine bottles and the champagne to sit on, so they don't drip on the wooden top. And then I think we're done. Oh no, the paper serviettes – they're in the sideboard too.'

With the last pieces in place Julia studied the table and the sideboard. 'We haven't got any nibbles to go with the drinks before dinner! Milton,' she called in the direction of the kitchen. 'I can go out and get some nuts and crackers to have with pre-dinner drinks.'

'It's all here - just have a look in the pantry. I bought a whole lot of stuff yesterday when I went to the supermarket.'

'God, he's so organised – he's really is good at this.' Linda poked a finger into Julia's side. 'As well as being good at a lot of other things, I'm sure.'

They looked at each other and burst out laughing, and Milton, who was just coming through the door, said, 'What's the joke?'

'Oh, please don't tell him! *Please* don't!' said Linda and blushed again. 'I think I've embarrassed myself enough for one day already.'

33

At the end of the afternoon, they sat down with a belated cup of coffee and a plate of biscuits in front of the fire. Outside the early winter darkness has shrouded the view from the big windows, but inside everything was warm and bright.

'We're all ready.' Julia looked around the room. 'Soon Linda and I will go and change and stay behind the scenes until everyone's arrived, well not Helen and company, but the others. I can't tell you how excited I am at the thought of watching all those surprised faces.'

Linda looked from one to the other and said slowly, 'I'm getting a feeling you're about to give me a surprise too – not that I can think what it would be, but Julia has that naughty look on her face.' She turned to Milton. 'Did you notice?'

'Naughty look?' said Milton with mock

surprise. 'What do you mean, naughty look? You must be confusing her with someone else.'

'I'm going to change in your room, if you don't mind,' said Julia when she and Linda walked down the glass passage towards the bedrooms. 'I don't want Milton to see the dress when I'm half in it and not ready. You might have to help with the zip at the back. I don't think I'll be able to reach it. I had to get the shop assistant to do it for me when I tried it on.'

Half an hour later Linda and Julia looked at each other and Linda said, 'You look stunning! Like a film star or something, Seb was totally right. I must get a photo of you to show him. Go and stand by that white door and I'll do it now. And Milton's going to fall to his knees when he sees you, just like I said when you showed us that dress in the mall.'

Milton didn't fall to his knees, but the way his eyes fixed on hers and the message she could read there was enough to tell Julia that he thought she looked amazing. 'My God, you're something else! Nobody would ever guess you're a mechanic.'

'Take that X-rated look off your face before you set the house on fire,' she whispered while Linda pretended she wasn't listening.

They surveyed what they had done, everything that had been set out, the chairs that had been moved to make room for fifteen people to circulate in the living room and around the dining table, then Milton said, 'If you two are going to make your surprise entrance without anybody spotting you I think you'd better go and hide in a bedroom right now. I just heard the beep the electronic monitor makes when a car turns into the drive.'

'Aha, that's how you know to open the door just as I reach for the doorbell.' Julia took Linda's hand and as they hurried down the passage towards the bedrooms there was a second little beep. They sat side by side on Linda's bed and tried to wait patiently until they imagined everyone had been introduced.

'There is one thing I can tell you,' said Julia. 'My sister Barb is married to Anthony, who's a consulting engineer for the sawmill. He specialises in automated machinery, the kind that involves computers and robotics. But Barb has never met Milton before, and she has no idea that I know him. So that's going to be fun. And the other family are very good friends of Milton's. I know them, but they don't know that I know him too. So, it's surprises all around, and then my best friend Helen and her husband and two sons will arrive - a bit later because I wanted the first two families to get over the introductions first. Helen has never even heard Milton's name, and she hasn't got the slightest idea I've been dating anyone, much less that I've got into a serious relationship. She's going to be outraged and tell me off in front of everyone, you just wait.' She laughed at the prospect; surprising Helen had been a sport since high school, but this would he biggest surprise ever.

And finally, when Julia thought that most of the guests would have a glass in their hands she and Linda walked down the passage together.

The reaction of those in the living room could not have been more gratifying. Barb's eyes opened wide, and she started saying something, and Seb shouted, 'Linda!' very loudly at exactly the same moment that his mother exclaimed, 'Julia!'

In Julia's mind two disembodied voices talked over each other as intermingled light blue and pale green washed briefly across her vision, and she smiled.

Milton pulled her close to his side with his arm over her shoulders and kissed her temple the way he often did, then turned so they both faced their guests.

'This is a surprise party,' he said. 'Julia and I are now officially a couple, but we thought it would be fun to see your reactions, seeing how many inter-connections there are in this room. I'll give you an outline, so you realise the complexity.'

The outline took nearly five minutes, despite how concise he tried to make it, as questions and comment came towards him from nearly everyone and the big room was filled with exclamations, hugs and laughter. Julia continued to stand next to Milton where she wanted to be when Helen and her family arrived. Half an hour later she noticed Linda walking towards the front door, though Julia hadn't heard the doorbell. She turned to Milton, who was talking to Anthony, stood on tiptoes with her hand on his shoulder and whispered close to his ear, 'Hold me, please!'

Without turning his head, he reached out and pulled her close just as Helen and Gordon walked into the room. A few minutes later Julia held her hand up in front of Helen's face, palm out like someone directing traffic and laughed. 'Enough questions! Let's go and find you a glass of something non-alcoholic and then you can talk to someone else for a while. You'll get the full disclosure later.'

'You are the most secretive person I've ever known,' said Helen and followed her towards the sideboard. 'I don't know how you could hold it in for so long.'

Interesting, thought Julia, that I never hear Helen's thoughts even when I know she's definitely thinking about me, something emotional and personal, like these last few minutes. I wonder why?

· · ·

'It's like a reunion,' said Gordon to Milton and Julia later that evening. 'I hadn't seen Anthony since I stopped playing squash ten years ago, so catching up with him was fun. And you and I met once at a stag night many years ago, Milton, when we were in our twenties. I think it was for that McMillan guy, what was his name, the one who became a body builder. And you're right, the inter-connections in this room are incredible. Someone should write a book about it.'

'Maybe somebody *is* writing a book about it.' Julia smiled at the look of surprise on Milton's face. She knew he would ask her to explain later and looked forward to telling him about her evening with Carol in all its glorious detail.

When the last guests left just after midnight the rain had stopped. They went back inside after saying a last goodbye and sat around the fire with a final glass of wine and the chocolates Linda had hidden in the sideboard.

'I had to,' she explained to Milton. 'The kids were going to demolish the lot before dinner. Seb and James discovered them as if by smell, and when I saw how many they were putting in their pockets I waited until they walked away and put the bowl in the sideboard and then I forgot about it!'

'Brilliant move!' He got to his feet. 'Let's put

our jackets on and go outside for a moment. There's something I want to show you two.'

With warm jackets on they headed for the front door, and Milton grabbed Linda's wrist when she reached for the light switch in the hall. 'No lights, we need our night vision. That's why I turned the living room lights off when we went to get our jackets. Light spilling out on that side would ruin it. Be careful to follow where I go, Linda – we're going to walk around the house in the dark.'

Outside he led the way around the side where his bedroom was, to where the lights from the sawmill didn't reach. In front of them the night sky was ablaze with stars that seemed impossibly close. The Milky Way was a swooping band of bright dots that seemed close enough to reach up and touch. With no houses anywhere near and the city hidden behind hills they felt like the only human beings on the planet.

'Oh my God!' said Julia. 'How glorious! What a fabulous surprise – thank you!'

34

FIVE MONTHS LATER

On a Sundy morning when spring was well underway after a harsh winter, Julia and Milton sat on the little deck outside their bedroom with a cup of coffee, and Julia turned her face to the sun with a sigh of contentment.

'Isn't it amazing how sitting out of the wind makes such a difference on a sunny day. I thought it would be too cold to sit outside, but here in this sheltered corner it's lovely.'

'A deliberate part of the design, very deliberate.' Milton gestured at the walls on two sides of the deck. 'It took a while to get it just right. Mark, the architect, who's a friend you haven't met yet – he lives in Wellington - he and I spent a lot of time discussing how to place the house, and it was quite tricky. For a start I wanted to have the view from a couple of key rooms like the living room and the bedroom and a sheltered corner facing the morning sun, and that corner had to be shielded from both the sight and the noise from the factory *and* from the prevailing wind. It's worked out really well. And then I decided that having the guest room and its en-suite bathroom in a separate wing would be a good idea and that gave me another sheltered corner.'

'The advantage of constructing a house out of big building blocks,' said Julia. 'You could move the blocks around and just angle the different parts however you wanted.'

'And Mark had the great idea of having little connecting passages which meant that we could spread the house out more, so it became a cluster of modules linked up more loosely. As he said, I have enough land to spread things out, so why not do it.'

Around the corner of the house came Linda in jeans and steel-capped boots, with her high-viz jacket on and a hard hat dangling from one hand.

'What are you doing here on a Sunday?' asked Julia in surprise. 'You're not working today are you?'

'I'm being an observer today with one of the maintenance guys. I was with the operations manager all week, but now that I think I'd rather be an engineer than a landscape architect I'm taking all the chances I get offered to find out how things work. But what's his name, the guy who picked me up this morning.' She looked at Milton. 'You know the big one who always looks as if he's wearing a hard hat that's too small for his head? He said to come and get you. There's something he wants to show you.'

Milton looked hard at Linda. 'That's Boris. Did he pick you up?'

She gave him a puzzled look. 'Yeah, he offered to. Why?'

'I'm not sure I want you in the nearly empty factory with Boris, or in his car for that matter.'

Now Linda looked surprised. 'Is there something about him that I should know?'

Milton sighed. 'Perhaps it's wrong to talk about his past, he's paid his dues to society as they say. But you need to know for your own protection. A few years ago, he was in prison for quite some time, convicted of two sexual assaults involving violence, quite a few years ago. I think he was about eighteen or nineteen at the time. And I really don't want you to be alone anywhere with him.'

'He' OK,' said Linda calmly. 'He really is - or else he doesn't fancy me, but he's not made the slightest move in that direction.' Then she laughed. 'And don't forget he knows that I'm kind of your adopted goddaughter or whatever. He wouldn't dare touch me.'

Milton frowned and turned to Julia. 'What do you think about this?'

'My first thought was that Linda's old enough to make up her own mind. And my second thought is I don't want her anywhere near the guy. She's too important to me.'

'But I have no choice,' said Linda reasonably. 'I have no transport to get here, so one of the guys picks me up on the way here every morning. I take the bus to the highway junction, and they pick me up from the bus shelter there. It's not like there's a bus all the way to this place. And the offer to spend some time watching Boris fixing things on a Sunday was just too good to miss.'

'I do think you need a car though,' said Julia. 'I don't know why I hadn't thought of it before. But to go back to your personal safety, I don't think anyone would dare do anything to you inside the factory seeing it's full of cameras. But to go in cars with all these different guys, particularly on the way home after an evening shift. I really don't like it.'

Linda laughed. 'You two are worrying about nothing, but OK, I'll start saving for a car. Could you come with me now, Milton? You really need to see this.'

Later that day, Milton more or less abducted Linda from the factory at midday and said she was having lunch with them, and he would drive her home.

'I'm going to buy Linda a car,' he said when he returned after taking Linda home. 'Something second hand with a good safety rating. If she does take up engineering studies she might want to come and work here every holiday, and we'll have this problem all the time. I know I'm being very particular about this, but I kind of feel like she's our pretend daughter, and I feel very close to her.'

'I was thinking just the same thing while I was sitting here reading when you were gone. I decided to find her something at the big car yard down Winslow Street. I know the guy who owns it and he'll let me take a car away and check it over. I'll buy it in my name and have her covered as a driver on the insurance, so she just pays for the fuel.'

'Great idea, but I don't mind buying it.' He looked absently at the view outside the big living room window for a moment and added, 'Isn't it strange how we both feel so connected to her? Before I met her I would never have thought I could develop a nearly father-type connection with a teenager I had just met.'

'I was the same.' Julie smiled up at him. 'Why don't you sit down. I'm getting a crick in my neck. One day not long after Linda moved in with me, we had a very interesting talk about her parents and their problems, and we got very close after that. And then I realised I knew how parents feel. You know - that anything that affected Linda would affect me, constantly thinking of what might happen and how to avoid it. And that tight connection infuses you with the feeling that you're totally responsible. So, the thought of her in a car with that possibly reformed sex-offender made me cringe with apprehension.' She looked seriously at Milton and said decisively, 'Let's buy a car this week, one with central locking and a five star safety rating and all the clever bits. I'll get onto it tomorrow.'

'Do you need to put this in front of her parents? I know you've talked to them a couple of times in the past.'

'No, Linda can tell them herself. I spoke to her parents a few weeks ago just to make sure they know she's decided to stay in my apartment and that I'm fine with it. They said they'll probably sign up for another two-year stint in Bangladesh after this one, with a month back here in between. Let's just pretend she's ours and do things for her. There's no need for her parents to know and start feeling guilty.'

And in her mind she saw a rapid wash of burgundy red accompanied that now familiar disembodied voice. *I love you, you wonderful woman.*

ONE YEAR LATER

The little beep from the electronic device at the gate alerted Milton to head for the front door. Before Linda had even got out of the black Volvo they had bought for her the previous year, three children spilled out of the car and ran towards Milton.

'We've been to the mall,' announced Debbie and held up a parcel. 'I got to choose the cakes. They're my favourites – chocolate peanut cookies.'

James rolled his eyes and Seb said, 'She only took about half an hour to decide what we should buy, and then she *still* picked the same as last time it was her turn *and* the time before.'

The children walked around Milton as if he were a traffic island and disappeared into the house, and Linda came up for her customary hug.

'They're very boisterous today, must be the

spring weather. It was like herding cats when we were in the mall.'

'I know the feeling,' said Julia, who had appeared beside them. 'Last time I took the three of them to the mall I discovered a new phenomenon – three children can disappear in four directions at once.'

'We could get their parents to insert luggage tracker tags under their skin.' Milton closed the door and led the way towards the noise coming from the kitchen. 'I think they're getting drinks out, let's go and see what they're doing.'

At the end of their visit James asked if Milton would take them into the factory again, something he did every time he came, but Milton said no. 'It's fine on a Sunday, but it's Saturday today, and I won't take you in there when the machinery is working until your heads are big enough for a hard hat to fit properly. The gantry cranes and all the machinery make it a dangerous place.'

'I have a hard hat at home – my bicycle helmet,' said Debbie. 'I'll bring it next time and then you can take me, and we'll leave the boys outside.'

'Hmm,' said Milton. 'Now what am I going to do? I suppose I'll have to take you. I never thought of bicycle helmets. But we'll stick to the elevated observation platforms, I think. Bring the helmets next time you come.'

They departed as noisily as they had arrived, arguing about whose turn it was to sit in the front with Linda, and left Julia and Milton laughing.

'Rather Linda than me,' said Julia. 'Having the three of them together in the car sometimes drives me mad. You can't finish a sentence, much less a conversation, without getting interrupted. But Seb got a chance to tell me in private that he's not going to marry Linda after all. He's fallen in love with a girl with freckles who plays the violin.'

Milton put arm over Julia's shoulders and pulled her close to his side. 'Aren't we lucky to have them? And aren't we lucky we can wave goodbye when they go back to their respective homes? A perfect arrangement.'

THANK YOU

We hope you've enjoyed reading this story and would consider leaving a review, or even a rating.

These are not only much appreciated, they also help other readers discover new authors.

For other titles from Lightpool Publishing, please read on.

ABOUT SASKIA

Saskia Woodhill is an emerging author or soft romance novels where slightly paranormal characters occasionally engage in outrageous behaviour and sometimes find themselves in funny or dangerous situations - or funny and dangerous at the same time. Stories that will make you laugh and cry and turn the pages to the satisfying ending.

ALSO FROM SASKIA

Alba's abrupt exit in the middle of an interview for a dream job sets off a chain of events she never saw coming. The inexplicable dread she occasionally feels isn't her imagination, it's a warning signal, one that others don't sense. But this time simply walking away wasn't enough - now a powerful man is determined to discover why she left.

Follow Alba on her intense, emotional journey of secrets, risk-taking and life-changing decisions into a world where the stakes are high, trust is precious, and her future hangs in the balance. This story will keep you riveted, questioning fate and the power of love.

Available from all good bookshops.

OTHER TITLES FROM
LIGHTPOOL PUBLISHING

Letters from the Past by Tina Clough is a series of stand-alone novels where a letter from or about the past reveals something that changes a woman's perceptions of her family, and affects her outlook on life. Life can change in a moment and sometimes you have to step into the unknown and take a chance on love.

Having had nobody in her life since her husband died, Lara unexpectedly finds herself involved with three men. One is planning to use her, one she plans to use for her own ends, and one becomes a "friend-with-benefits" with surprising results. Sometimes a quiet schoolteacher is not all she seems at first glance.

Callista experiences an event of apparent ESP at the Okehampton Castle ruins and becomes a media sensation, but the effect it has on her life is dramatic. How do two people, one calm. one seriously claustrophobic, who feel they are poles apart, cope for an hour and a half in total darkness in a stalled lift? And can they handle the consequences?

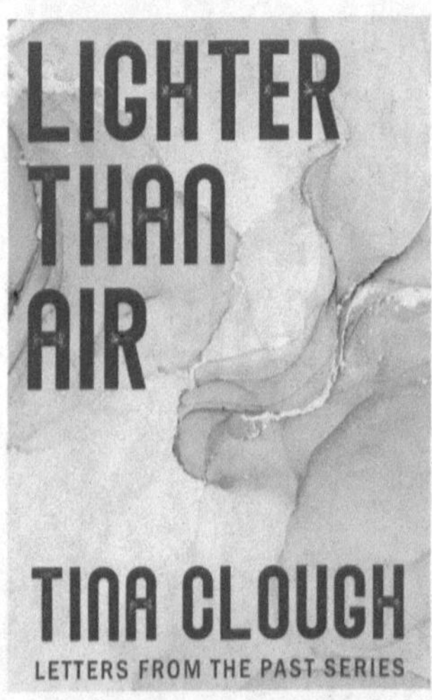

Sofia's life is in turmoil: a difficult diva mother, a letter with a confession about a family killing and having to accept help from a man she loathes when she is injured. Can reluctant attraction turn into love?

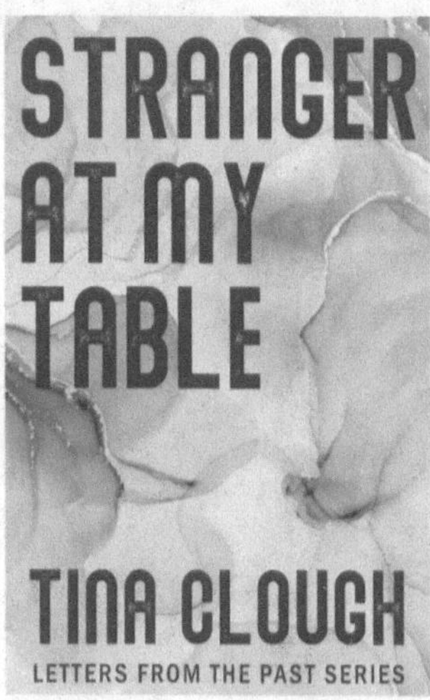

Who is the stranger living in the empty house Miranda inherited from her grandmother? Why is he living like a secretive recluse in someone else's house? Reckless Miranda decides to confront him, and what she discovers prompts her to set out on a fearless quest to bring justice to a man who has given up hope. But is the gamble too great or a risk worth taking?

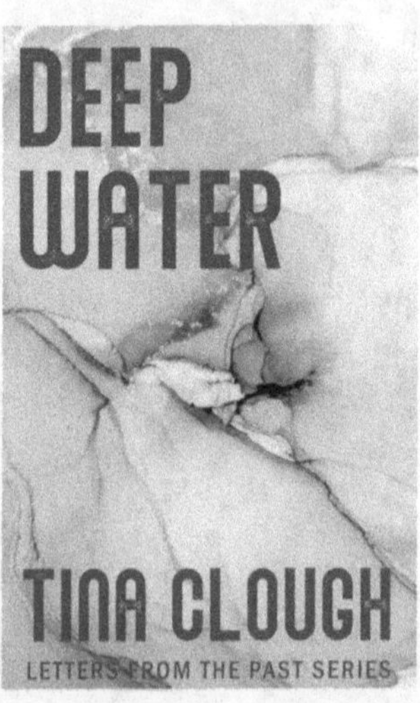

When Emma finds an old letter in a library book she is instantly intrigued, but by researching the origin of the letter she unwittingly opens the door to danger and becomes the target for threats and harassment. Nearly desperate, she takes a leap of blind faith into the unknown and accepts an offer of help from a stranger - but can she trust him?

Jamie, an ardent protester against the gigantic Vista Resort development and Leo Masters, the high-powered developer, seem unlikely to ever agree on anything. But unexpected coincidences and chance brings them together in a fragile state of mutual respect. Will courage and kindness resolve the situation, or do they need help?

After a bizarre accident with ESP overtones, the media haunt Arapera. But can she trust an offer of help from a man she has only met once? Or will she regret it for the rest of her life if she doesn't take the chance? Sometimes life is a knife-edge balance between staying safe and taking risks, and there is no way of predicting if the gamble is worth it.

When crime-writer Saskia finds an unconscious stranger, she has a strange and strong emotional connection. Pretending to be his cousin and with no thought for the consequences, she spends weeks at his hospital bedside. But what will happen when he wakes and discovers she has invaded his life, breached his privacy and made crucial decisions on his behalf?

THE GIRL WHO LIVED TWICE

What would you do if you woke up one morning and found that time had rewound exactly a year? Would you revisit your past mistakes and try to do better? Would you try to get revenge on those who had wronged you? Or would you use what you knew to get rich? When Mia finds herself in her own past, she must decide how best to use her pre-knowledge of one year's worth of events and personal issues.

www.ingramcontent.com/pod-product-compliance
Lightning Source LLC
Chambersburg PA
CBHW011131190726

48289CB00012B/2994